WHO'S AFRAID OF MERYL STREEP?

CANCELLED
BY
PENZANCE LIBRARY
MORRAB GDNS.

MODERN MIDDLE EAST

LITERATURES IN TRANSLATION SERIES

WHO'S AFRAID OF MERYL STREEP?

RASHID AL-DAIF

TRANSLATED BY

PAULA HAYDAR

AND NADINE SINNO

CENTER FOR MIDDLE EASTERN STUDIES

UNIVERSITY OF TEXAS AT AUSTIN

This English translation copyright © 2014
by the Center for Middle Eastern Studies
at The University of Texas at Austin.

All rights reserved
Printed in the United States of America

Translators: Paula Haydar and Nadine Sinno
Cover art: © 2006 iStock, Shauni

Cover and text design: Kristi Shuey
Series Editor: Wendy E. Moore

Library of Congress Control Number: 2014949553
ISBN: 978-0-292-76307-4

Originally published in Arabic as *Tiṣṭifil Meryl Streep*
(Beirut: Riad El-Rayyes Books, 2001).

Everyone knows the saying about not judging a book by its cover. In Arabic the saying is a little different: "*Yuʿrafu al-maktūbu min ʿunwānihi,*" or "The book is known by its title." Though the two sayings don't match up word for word, the idea is clear: for better or for worse, the title is a significant component of a book. It provides the potential reader with a first impression, encourages or discourages the opening of the first page, and it is also what lingers in the memory after the last page is turned.

Rashid al-Daif is a prolific novelist whose wide readership has undoubtedly been drawn into reading his stories not only by their interesting and relevant themes and plots—and al-Daif's unique narrative voice and literary style—but also, to a large extent, by the novelty of his titles. Take, for example, titles like *Ghaflat al-Turāb* [The nodding off of the earth/soil/ground] (1991), or *Nāḥiyat al-Barā'a* [The side/point of view of innocence] (1997), or *Insay al-Sayyāra* [Forget the car] (2002), and even *Learning English* (1998), whose novelty lies in the phonetic spelling in Arabic script: "Lirningh Inghlish." Each of al-Daif's titles piques the interest of a potential reader by invoking an image or an idiom that is at once familiar and incomprehensible, causing him or her to wonder what it really means. *Tiṣtifil Meryl Streep* is certainly no exception to this rule, and this title provides an excellent starting point for discussing some of the particular challenges al-Daif's novels pose for his translators. For the Arabic reader, the title *Tiṣtifil Meryl Streep* is both catchy and intriguing, but for the translator it is, to say the least, elusive and tantalizing. *Meryl Streep* is immediately recognizable on a global scale, of course, even when spelled out in Arabic script, but it is that first word, *Tiṣtifil*, that has been the source of many an hour of discussion and frustration. In a nutshell, it is a translator's nightmare. The reasons for this are many, but primarily the problem stems from the difficulty in capturing not only the exact meaning of the colloquialism *Tiṣtifil* but also its tone, especially without the luxury of the larger context in which it is being said. A Lebanese reader, or any Arab reader for that matter, will immediately recognize the word since she or he is a seasoned member of the sociolinguistic community and cultural context in which it is spoken. In common usage, the phrase, which is primarily spoken among friends or by an elder to a younger person (and not usually the other way around), means "Go ahead, do as you like," "Whatever you want," "Do as you please," "Suit yourself," and more often than not it is said with a slightly derisive tone, possibly with some exasperation as well—though it is nonetheless ultimately a playful and friendly expression said with a shrug, a nod, and a smile. Hidden inside the word is the root *ṭifl*, meaning "child" or "baby," giving rise to connotations in meaning suggesting that the person to whom the expression is said is being told to "Go ahead, placate yourself," "Baby yourself," "Follow your whims like a child." It is important to note that in al-Daif's title, *Tiṣṭifil Meryl Streep*, the expression *Tiṣṭifil* is not being said directly *to* Meryl Streep. If the title meant to say, "Do what *you* like, Meryl Streep," or "Suit yourself, Meryl Streep," the verb would be in the direct imperative form, with feminine suffix: "*Iṣṭifli ya* Meryl Streep." Rather, in its form as a third-person feminine verb, the phrase means "Meryl Streep does what she likes," or better, "Meryl Streep *can do* what she likes," or "*Let* Meryl Streep do what she likes."

References to the novel in English-language articles and scholarship on Rashid al-Daif have often translated the title *Tiṣṭifil Meryl Streep* as "To Hell with Meryl Streep." While this title has its merits and would certainly serve to draw the attention of a potential English-language reader, its imprecision and mismatched (and misdirected) tone have given us pause as the novel's translators. In the context of the novel, the narrator is charmed by Meryl Streep and becomes bewildered while watching *Kramer vs. Kramer* on satellite TV. Even without subtitles, he is captured by the film, attempts to understand the plot, and becomes enamored with the heroine while simultaneously feeling threatened by what he sees as women's liberation gone too far. Because he is watching the film alone in his apartment after he has become estranged from his own wife, he cannot help but project Meryl Streep's actions onto her. It is at this point, roughly midway through the novel, that the narrator says, "*Tiṣṭifil* Meryl Streep!" and goes on to express his disgust with

his observation that while women in the West act out and portray
notions of freedom, independence, and liberation in movies, it
is the women in the East (i.e., his wife) who actually carry them
out in reality! When he exclaims, "*Tiṣṭifil* Meryl Streep!" he means
"Fine, let Meryl Streep do as she pleases, but why should *our* women
(*my* woman) behave that way?" In other words, what's fine for the
West is fine for the West, but what's it got to do with *us*? The anger
in his tone is directed at his wife and her breach with traditional
norms and traditional gender roles, not at Meryl Streep. His anger
is not only directed at the West for introducing modern ways to the
East, but also, and perhaps more poignantly, at the East and the
Eastern woman in particular for daring to change and to disturb his
traditional Arab male psyche and dominance.

This particular title, then, is intriguing to the Arabic reader
from the outset because it uses an everyday idiom, but it is not clear
in what context "Let Meryl Streep do what she likes" is being said.
The title sticks in the reader's mind and becomes fully charged with
meaning over the course of the novel. When the narrator repeats
the exact words of the title in his interior monologue, it becomes
a thematic lightning rod through which the novel's and narrator's
major conflicts are expressed.

After many discussions and long consideration, after proposing
one translation of the title after another, such as "Forget Meryl
Streep," and "The Hell with Meryl Streep," and "Meryl Streep
Can Do What She Likes," and "What's Meryl Streep Got to Do with
It?," and "You're No Meryl Streep!," we settled on the title "Who's
Afraid of Meryl Streep?" While this translation clearly steers away
from attempting to recast the actual words used in the original title
and is a kind of translator's "leap," the resonance with a culturally
familiar allusion to Edward Albee's *Who's Afraid of Virginia Woolf?*
(1962) provides a compelling level of compensation for the loss. We
felt it to be a good solution that is effective on a number of levels.
First, because of the proximity to the title of Albee's acclaimed
play, it is catchy and has a good ring to it. Also, association with the
play (and with the historic literary/cultural figure Virginia Woolf
herself) immediately conjures Albee's themes of strained marital
relationships and conflicting views of men and women toward each

other's changing societal and sexual roles, themes that are also brought into sharp focus in al-Daif's novel. Just as the couple in the novel can be seen as a distorted copy of the failed marriage in *Kramer vs. Kramer*, it also bears resemblance to the breakdown of Martha and George's marriage. Furthermore, as one reads the novel, he or she will quickly discover that it is indeed the narrator who is afraid of Meryl Streep and the "big, bad wolf" she represents within the context of the novel.

In *Who's Afraid of Meryl Streep?* al-Daif masterfully employs his most-preferred novelist's tool, the first-person narrator, which he described in a 2008 speech delivered at the Second International Forum on the Novel in Lyon, France, as "a lever; a worker's tool; a mighty instrument that allows me to put myself inside the skin of some other character I would not want to be, and allows me to adopt his logic and see with his eyes." Al-Daif is so skilled at using this tool to give the impression the story in the novel took place in his own past, "as if it were the most personal and intimate account of my own life," that some Arab reviewers expressed their shock and disbelief that the author could describe his own wife in such a shameless manner. However, despite the difficulty separating fact from fiction that some readers may have, al-Daif's narrative style certainly succeeds in allowing us to "spy through the keyhole and see what is going on behind closed doors," thus satisfying our hidden human tendency toward voyeurism. In *Who's Afraid of Meryl Streep?* al-Daif combines the first-person narrator strategy with his often-stated belief that "the bed is the place where the modern West and the "traditional" East confront each other, often violently." And while Rashoud, the novel's narrator and protagonist, is not Rashid al-Daif, the author al-Daif does envision Rashoud as a character who nevertheless "resembles the majority" of his countrymen, as he explained to his audience at the Second International Forum on the Novel. Likewise, the female characters in his novels "are like millions of Arab women," and Rashoud's wife is no exception. In *Who's Afraid of Meryl Streep?* al-Daif puts images under a magnifying lens—ill-conceived images held by Westerners of both Eastern and Western women and men as well as by Easterners of both Eastern and Western women and men—forcing us all to question these images and come to terms with the often appalling sentiments and behavior of the novel's characters, most notably on the battlefield of the bedroom.

What, then, is our narrator, Rashoud, *really* afraid of, and how does he deal with his fears of a modern Lebanon that remains caught between tradition and modernity? In her intriguing study of the exploration of modernity and modernization in contemporary Arabic fiction, Samira Aghacy uses one of al-Daif's novels, *ʿAzīzī al-Sayyid Kawabata* (1995) [translated by Paul Starkey as *Dear Mr. Kawabata* (1999)], as a primary text because of "its obsession with modernity" (2006: 561). She concludes "the narrative underlines the importance of technological advancement but insists on adherence to a hoary patriarchal tradition against the chaotic tide of change and on seeing women as bearers of tradition who ensure protection from the threat of cultural invasion and appropriation" (2006: 576). This ethos, this love-hate relationship with modernity, continues to occupy a significant presence in both al-Daif novels that followed *Dear Mr. Kawabata—Nāḥiyat al-Barāʾa* (1997) [translated by Paula Haydar as *This Side of Innocence* (2001)] and *Lirningh Inghlish* (1998) [translated by Paula and Adnan Haydar as *Learning English* (2007)]—and reaches a fever pitch in *Who's Afraid of Meryl Streep?*, published in 2001. In this novel, what the narrator finds at stake in the face of modernity are his public image, his masculinity, and his way of life. From its opening pages, the novel suggests that it is the narrator's unnamed wife who primarily threatens his sense of masculinity and causes him anxiety. She must be cajoled, disciplined, and even punished into upholding the narrator's standards of morality and proper social behavior. The newlywed Rashoud, whose name represents the nickname of the author's first name "Rashid" (and the name of the main protagonist in many of al-Daif's novels), prides himself for being ahead of his times in terms of his progressive thinking and his embracing of all things modern, including cable television, where "in a split second, the viewer would be transported from the Middle Ages to ages that have not even occurred yet and from places of worship to bars and nightclubs" (p. 1). Rather than rely on his in-laws for cable television, he is set on buying his

1 own TV and a cable subscription, hoping that the television will brighten up the new home, win over his emotionally and sexually distant wife, and make her more responsive to his sexual advances and affection.

However, despite Rashoud's infatuation with technological advancement and despite his self-proclaimed progressive thinking on many issues, such as freedom of speech and religious coexistence, he still believes firmly in a restricted type of modernity, one that keeps women in a subdued relationship with men and holds them up to strict moral codes that are based on patriarchal cultural customs and religious scripture. For Rashoud, a woman's body as well as her mind must be preserved in a state of purity and innocence until her husband deflowers her and introduces her to the joys of the flesh. Like many of his friends, the narrator has no qualms about voicing his double standards regarding premarital sex. While he understands that a woman may have some kind of physical relationship with a man prior to getting married, he insists that "that physical contact must be within boundaries" (p. 105). He insists that "a man should receive his wife's body in perfect condition," and that a woman's chastity "is a precious gift for a husband, one that will continue to affect him forever because it solidifies the bond between them as husband and wife, keeping this bond unbreakable" (p. 105). Like his friend, he firmly believes that he "get[s] to deflower at least one" and that it is quite simply his "right" (p. 57). It is no surprise, then, that when Rashoud suspects that his wife had had premarital sexual encounters, he feels deeply betrayed and his whole world— his moral compass of right and wrong—is completely shattered. He goes on a quixotic quest to find out if, when, how, with whom, and how often his wife might have engaged in sexual relations. His tragicomic adventures in the search for the "truth" take many forms, including coercing his wife to surrender to a medical examination that amounts to a virginity test, interrogating her incessantly and invasively about her past, and even examining her private parts while she is sleeping to determine the likelihood of her having engaged in anal sex prior to marrying him. Of course, his efforts remain fruitless and only serve to add to his sense of anxiety, neurosis, and helplessness.

While Rashoud holds his wife to the highest standards of morality and expects her and other women to bear the responsibility of upholding traditional values and mores, he does not hold himself or his fellow men to the same standards of behavior. Nor does he try to do his part in preserving the conservative values of a society that, in his mind, has exceeded the West in its tolerance of depravity. Rather, he preys on women who cross his path, including a seamstress in whose eyes he detects an abnormal level of sexual curiosity and longing. When he attempts to seduce the seamstress, he finds himself facing a huge scandal with her brothers, who beat him up, grope his wife in front of the neighbors, and threaten to kill him if he does not compensate for his actions by paying them an exorbitant sum of money. In a scene that echoes Meryl Streep's actions in *Kramer vs. Kramer*, Rashoud's wife turns her back on him without thinking twice and files for divorce—a punishment that, according to him, in no way fits the crime.

Despite his misogynistic tendencies, however, al-Daif's protagonist is depicted as a byproduct of his society, as a tormented individual trying so hard to fit in a Lebanese society that is still attempting to figure out its place in the world. In other words, he is himself a victim of a society that is both old-fashioned and modernized. On the one hand, it allows women some of the most progressive rights in the Middle East. On the other hand, this same society is not quite ready to detach a man's sense of masculinity from his ability to keep the women in his life in check. While al-Daif himself may never use the term "performative" to describe the functioning of gender in his novel, the narrative itself begs for a gender analysis. The narrative is fraught with instances of men and women performing—or subverting—gender roles. According to Judith Butler, gender is "not a noun, but neither a set of free-floating categories"; rather, "the substantive effect of gender is performatively produced and compelled by the regulatory practices of gender coherence" (1990: 24). Rashoud is constantly trying to *construct* himself as a "good Arab man," one whom he still perceives as someone who provides for and protects his wife, satisfies her sexually, and keeps her under his thumb. He has internalized the dominant culture's prescriptions of a manly man, and he strives toward that male ideal. And when he fails, he is pained by his shortcomings. For instance, Rashoud constantly worries about being ridiculed for and emasculated by his wife's actions in front of other people. As seen in the above reference to his friends' views on sexuality, the narrator constantly refers to his macho friends when validating his stance on virginity and proper female and male behavior. When his wife leaves the house, he is primarily terrified of what people will think. Will they see him as an impotent, weak man?

> One thing I would not put up with was people saying that my wife walked out the door whenever she pleased as if I wasn't there. Neither would I allow people to say I didn't "satisfy" her or "provide" her with everything her heart desired. Rumor had it among my buddies that a wife whose husband "satisfied" her—sexually, of course—and "provided" everything she needed couldn't possibly object to anything. (p. 35)

The irony is, of course, that Rashoud can condemn and protest his wife's actions, but he can do very little to police her, let alone bring her back home. His wife, a woman of few words and big deeds, dominates him. She, too, performs gender in a male-dominated society, but her acts are often extremely subversive of traditional gender norms. That Rashoud's wife is portrayed as a strong woman who is not afraid to speak her mind, engages in sexual transgressions, defies her husband, and ultimately leaves her marriage shows the limitations of holding on to rigid gender roles in an ever-evolving Lebanon. Indeed, Rashoud finds himself disarmed and disillusioned in a globalized Lebanon that has witnessed the shifting of gender roles, not just the proliferation of new media and information technology. At the end of the novel, he fails to live up to his traditional ideals of masculinity *and* he loses a wife—one who, in his mind, was not even a "paragon of beauty," and should have felt lucky to be proposed to by a man like himself (p. 7). His is a bitter loss because he loses (and loses to) a "whore, daughter of a whore, descendant of generations of whores," the woman who, in a moment of rage, instead of accepting his semen "like a holy receptacle," spits it back in his mouth in an ultimate act of subversion and parody (p. 107).

While Rashoud himself might project an inflated sense of self, al-Daif keeps him in check by portraying him as a humbled man, one who must either come to terms with reality and the "New World Order" or find himself attacking windmills. This textual tension between seriousness and jest is established through the narrative's reliance on verbal and dramatic irony, wit, self-deprecating humor, and overall playfulness with the language—in typical al-Daif fashion. In his fascinating study of another of al-Daif's novels that deals with gender and sexuality, *'Awdat al-Almānī ilā Rushdih* (*How the German Came to His Senses*), Ken Seigneurie praises al-Daif's "delicate equivocation between candor and self-irony," which he sees as a "hallmark" of the author's war novels (2010: 48). Al-Daif's characters often elicit and demand a complicated response from the reader because, in their brutal honesty, they do not exclude themselves from criticism and ridicule. On the contrary, they willingly expose their deepest fears, insecurities, and yes, follies, to any discerning reader who is willing to listen.

Rashoud's trials and tribulations in *Who's Afraid of Meryl Streep?* invite numerous questions and discussions about the evolving and puzzling nature of gender and sexuality in Lebanon, the globalized Middle East, and elsewhere in the world. Is it truly acceptable for women to be on an equal footing with men when it comes to their premarital sexual experiences? To what extent are the notions of liberation and feminism Western constructs, and to what extent are they part and parcel of any modern society where men and women must grapple with shifting world views and social institutions? What are the limitations of modernity in a country like Lebanon that, on the one hand, prides itself for being one of the region's strongest democracies and most liberal countries, and on the other, continues to stigmatize premarital sex and is a place where reconstructive hymen surgery remains prevalent? Rashid al-Daif's novel does not shy away from asking these questions. As Rashoud finds himself sinking deeper and deeper into the abyss of self-doubt and uncertainty, so do we remain perplexed and eager for answers that are yet to be determined.

NOTE ON THE TRANSLATION

Our translation of *Tiṣṭifil Meryl Streep* was a truly collaborative effort that involved a series of long-distance, back and forth translation and editing, five pages at a time. It was the first of its kind for both of us. We enjoyed collaborating on translating this novel for many reasons. We had great "work chemistry" as colleagues, which is a necessary condition for any collaborative work—let alone one that involves comprehending, interpreting, and making decisions about another person's work of art. It meant taking turns nitpicking each other's translations until we were both satisfied with the final product. Our two voices had to be woven into one coherent voice that pledged allegiance to the source and target languages and cultures. It helped that we, Haydar and Sinno, had the same priority when it came to translation: we wanted to create an English-written text that lets the beauty, idiosyncrasy, and even callousness of al-Daif's language shine through—without falling into the trap of blind adherence to the original that often results in awkward or stilted prose. We thus attempted the balancing act of creating a translation that sounded idiomatic in English while still retaining the flavor of the Arabic; one that sounded perfectly at home in English but also stubbornly resisted "passing" as a text that was originally written in English. We believe that we were able to find this balance in part because one of us is a native speaker of Arabic, the other of English, and we have both lived and become culturally at home in Lebanon and the United States. We hope that our translation reflects our intimate knowledge of and deep affection for both Arabic and English language and culture.

We sought to create a translation that is loyal to the original without being enslaved by it or overly concerned with a word for word rendition—one that flows naturally and is accessible to native speakers of English, but at the same time does not sacrifice the spirit of the original Arabic. To that effect, we aimed for a tone that is neither too "high" nor too "low" in its register, but that rather mirrors the original in its moderate level of formality. We also avoided cumbersome glossaries and footnotes by translating all terms for which we found appropriate equivalents in English.

Whenever we did not translate an Arabic or French word into English, it was because the untranslated word was culturally significant, had made its way into the larger English lexicon, or because it was particularly important to keep it "foreign" for thematic or stylistic purposes. We made sure to embed the meaning of those foreign words in the text itself, such that the reader would not be at a loss. We trust that our readers will enjoy encountering some words in Arabic and French as it allows them to gauge not only the linguistic texture of Arabic but also the author's intended effects in creating a narrative that engages with three languages—Arabic, English, and French—thus manifesting the linguistic effect of globalization in modern Lebanon.

We must note that some of the graphic scenes in the novel gave us pause (to say the least), and we worked diligently to recreate them in a way that was as tasteful as possible. We cannot say that it was always possible to remain "tasteful," as the original text sometimes defied our squeamishness and demanded that we quell our reservations. For readers who might be faint of heart with regard to sexually explicit scenes, we express our sincerest empathy and assure them that we too sometimes found ourselves outside our comfort zones. Our consolation is that the daring scenes in the narrative are by no means gratuitous and that they truly contribute to illuminating character, plot, and theme. We have no doubt that they will spark intriguing and honest discussions of sex, gender, and sexuality.

References

Aghacy, Samira. "Contemporary Lebanese Fiction: Modernization without Modernity." *International Journal of Middle East Studies* 38 (2006): 561–580.

Albee, Edward. *Who's Afraid of Virginia Wolf?* New York: Signet, 1962.

Butler, Judith. *Gender Trouble: Feminism and the Subversion of Identity.* New York: Routledge, 1990.

al-Daif, Rashid. "Je: un levier" and "Le lit: un lieu de confrontation." Conference Presentation at the Second International Forum on the Novel, Lyon, France, May 26, 2008.

Seigneurie, Ken. "Irony and Counter-Irony in Rashid al-Daif's *How the German Came to His Senses.*" *College Literature* 37 (2010): 38–60.

WHO'S AFRAID OF MERYL STREEP?

I did not see the president of the United States, George Bush, announce the birth of the "New World Order" at home on my own television. I saw it at my in-laws', where my wife and I had been spending almost every evening since we got married.

We did not own a television early in our marriage because we had decided to buy the essentials first: the bedroom before anything else, then the stove and fridge, the living room furniture, and some curtains—since the apartment we rented did not have shutters and was heavily exposed to the sunlight and the neighbors' eyes, which were constantly directed at us, the newlyweds.

My in-laws had cable, which got them about eighty national and international stations that broadcasted an unfathomable number of shows and movies twenty-four hours a day. It was such a variety of programs that were so different in every way—in subject, form, color, language—and especially in customs and morals. In a split second, the viewer would be transported from the Middle Ages to ages that have not even occurred yet and from places of worship to bars and nightclubs. And, of course, there was CNN, where we followed live scenes of the second Gulf War (1991) and the minute-by-minute bombing of Iraq.

Truth be told, that night I had not been paying close attention to what the president was saying, and I did not even notice when he used the expression "New World Order" because I am simply incapable of watching and listening at the same time. I can either listen or watch. This problem was fairly manageable when all you used to see on the TV screen was the anchorman's head and chest, but it became impossible for me to follow the events when they started reporting them with the commentator invisible behind the screen. That kind of thing went way over my head because I could neither listen to what the commentator was saying nor really see what was being shown in front of me. As my wife had said, it was as if I was driving a car that sped up when you hit the brakes, instead of stopping—I was completely baffled. It reminded me of my dad. Whenever he listened to the radio, he would hold it right up to his ear and forbid us from talking so he could concentrate on what he was hearing and later—after the newsflash was over—he would pull the radio away from his ear and ask us, "What did he just say?" He did not have any hearing problems, so we would all burst into laughter without the least bit of shame or consideration like bad boys did in elementary school books in the old days in stories designed to teach children how *not* to behave. My dad would stand there, a faint smile across his face. I used to think the problem I was suffering from was typical of the older generation, old folks still unfamiliar with new technology, but apparently whatever applied to that generation applied to me as well since I could not get used to such contraptions either.

I have no idea why my mother-in-law once said to me, "You really like TV, Rashoud, don't you?" Did I really look that enamored by the TV? Her comment was strange because if it were up to me, I would not spend so much time in front of the television. It was my wife who forced me to watch. Perhaps my mother-in-law was trying to imply the opposite—that I did not really like TV and was not drawn enough to it during those crucial times, and that I had the wrong attitude.

To be honest, the other reason I had not paid attention to what President Bush was saying had nothing to do with my non-multitasking nature. I had been preoccupied by the fact that my wife refused to sleep at our house and would insist on staying at her parents' house, where she felt more secure and at home than in any other place. When I pleaded with her to go to our house, she said, "If you miss it so much, go spend the night there by yourself." It was not really the house I was missing. I was missing her, and I could not enjoy her except at home because we did not have as much freedom at her parents' house. Her mom woke up at the slightest movement, and the bed we slept on made noises every time we moved, so my wife would use that as an excuse to discourage my advances. My wife did not need me to clarify or profess any of this. She knew very well why I insisted on going home. Yet, despite all that, I still told her, "I don't miss the house. I miss you."

"We just slept together," she said. By that she meant that we had "slept" together in the afternoon before going to her parents' house.

"I can't get enough of you," I said.

"I've had more than enough."

With this last missile, she seemed to imply very dangerous things, though at the time I heard what I wanted to hear or what the circumstances permitted.

The afternoon she referred to, she had not been in the mood for sex. I kept insisting until she finally succumbed, though without actively participating. With her hand, she got me where I wanted to go and was irate when she realized I had been watching her closely as she skillfully evaded my fluid as if it were pure filth. The way she did that had given me the impression she was highly experienced at these things. After that incident, which she called "sleeping together," I wanted her twice as much. Instead of calming down, I had been aroused like never before. It was as if that mode of pleasure had brought back those premarital feelings of deprivation, when there was no woman at hand—and when, even if a woman did come along, I had no place of my own to enjoy her—so I would have to resort to such means for compensation.

When my wife came out of the bedroom dressed in her pajamas, thus declaring her decision to stay at her parents' house, I almost ravaged her with desire. I bombarded her with hugs and kisses and caresses, which made her mother uncomfortable. However, instead of giving us some privacy to do our own thing, her mother doubled the time she spent with us and would not leave the two of us alone.

It was strange since she had not been like that whenever I visited her daughter before we got married.

So, yes, that night I had not paid much attention to President George Bush's expression, and it did not occur to me that it would turn out to have such a historical significance. Later, I read in the local Lebanese media and heard on official Arabic channels and foreign Arabic-language news networks, especially the London news network, that President Bush had used this expression in his speech and that this expression defined the upcoming era, across the globe—and that that era was potentially going to last for scores, even hundreds, of years.

I had witnessed a historical moment without realizing it.

4   I also remember being preoccupied as I watched the television screen by the fact that President Bush's voice did not fit his appearance or position. It seemed to me that what was coming out of his mouth was not his own voice but rather the voice of someone else, a much smaller man who was the size of a marble and who resided in the president's throat. I had the impression that President Bush was merely moving his lips to make it seem as if he himself was making those sounds. President Bush's voice did not fit his appearance or his position or his responsibilities as the president of a great nation that had just achieved a final victory over the great USSR with its invincible armies. In my mind, the master of the universe and the leader of the planet should have a different voice, one befitting his rank and one coming directly out of his own mouth. It is interesting that Bill Clinton, the president who succeeded him, had some obvious voice issues as well.

One time, in an attempt to break the silence that settled in between my wife and me as we both sulked—I because I was feeling powerless, and she because she had no choice but to overpower me—I asked her, "Do you like how it sounds?"

As usual, she responded with one of her unpredictable comebacks. "You think your TV sounds better?"

I was not criticizing the sound of her mother's television, which actually was fuzzy at times. I was asking her what she thought of Bush's voice, how his voice sounded to her.

I had to buy a TV immediately, and I had to be decisive this time. I could not stall any longer because I had to put an end to her excuses for staying at her mother's house or for saying, "This house is empty."

She had even gone further than that. "It's like a graveyard," she once said.

What she had said was downright wrong. Perhaps our house felt gloomy because there was no TV, but comparing our house to a graveyard was unacceptable no matter what. That day I raised my voice and scolded her. Yes, I scolded her.

I told her that what she said was deplorable. "That's just haram," I insisted. "It's blasphemous."

She felt ashamed and went into our bedroom. She locked herself inside and cried for one long hour. I could hear her sobbing. After she had calmed down and come out of the room, I went to her and hugged her, and I apologized. She did not respond, and she did not lay her head on my shoulder to assure me that she was satisfied and had accepted my apology. But I felt that my apology had moved her deeply. That alone was enough for me to forgive her. Still, despite my forgiving her, I could never see any justification for saying such a thing. Comparing our house to a graveyard was shocking, and it struck me as a bad omen, an early sign of impending disaster. This was exactly what happened in the end—unless one does not consider life and marriage and unborn babies sacred.

I had to buy a television immediately, not only for my wife's sake, but because I was missing out on everything. It was on the television screen that history, geography, and the entire universe—the universe that was unfolding with all its secrets—were taking place. I had felt so left out the year before during the solar eclipse. All the television stations, the entire media, urged people not to leave their houses during the solar eclipse for fear they would go blind from staring at the sun as it disappeared behind the moon. And, sure enough, everybody stayed home and watched the solar eclipse from the comfort of their couches, except for me, because I simply did not have a television. I went out and started roaming the empty streets of Beirut, which were normally crowded. I felt so suffocated and on edge that I was ready to attack someone any minute.

When from a distance I spotted a young man carefully observing the view from his doorstep, I yelled at him: "Pull your head back inside!" I ran at him, ready to tackle him, so he pulled his head in and slammed the door. I kept heading toward the door, yelling at him. Then I heard his mother yell at him and call him a stubborn and wicked boy for putting himself, his siblings, and her in harm's way. Then she must have thrown something at him, but it missed him and hit the door. I glanced at the sun as it disappeared behind the moon, and my eyes teared up. Then I looked at it again as it appeared on the other side of the moon, and my eyes teared up again. I was worried I had caused some damage to my eyes, which I regretted. I resented myself immensely for my way of life, for my self-negligence. Why didn't I have a wife and kids with whom I could watch the eclipse as it occurred in Lebanon and all over the world from the comfort of my home, on my own TV? After the eclipse, I had nothing to tell people, while everybody else was so full of stories they didn't know where to start. What could I tell them when I hadn't seen anything? When I had spent that historical moment— the last solar eclipse in the second millennium AD—panicking over the disappearance of sunlight in the middle of the day and over the sight of Beirut's streets so empty and its windows shut so tightly as if atomic dust had started sprinkling down the day before and now blanketed the entire city.

I did not think twice about the brand of television I was going to buy: it had to be Sony. I told the storekeeper I wanted a *real* Sony because I knew very well (come on—I live in Lebanon) that "Sony" was being manufactured in various Asian countries like Taiwan and Malaysia and that it was being sold as if it were the real thing. A real Sony was more expensive, of course, and I made sure the store owner did not try to sell me a fake one for the price of a real one. I asked him for proof, and he pointed to a button and said that on a fake Sony that button would be located on the right, not the left. And when I asked him to show me a fake one, he said he would never let such a thing enter his store. He showed me other brands such as Philips and Grundig and Gold Star, among others, but I was adamant: I wanted a Sony! It is true that European brands are generally good quality, especially the German ones, but power is so erratic in our part of the world that it never stabilizes at 220 volts, so getting a Sony was a must since it was designed for such conditions. During the Lebanese civil war, people who owned Sony televisions would use them for lighting inside their houses when the power voltage was limited to 70 or 80 watts because with such low voltage light bulbs were not sufficient. The electricity situation nowadays is sometimes reminiscent of those times. Plus, I believe that all things electronic should be left to the Japanese. Their reputation in these things is as good as gold, and they have surely earned it. More importantly, I did not want to give my wife the satisfaction of being able to ask me, "Why didn't you get something better?" I was right. The first thing she said to me later was, "Sony is the best!"

The night before I bought the television, as I pressed my body against her, I gently found my way to the bare parts of her body without waking her. After I came back from rinsing off, I found her awake. She asked me, "Why are you still up?" I told her I was rinsing off, and she asked why. When I told her why, she said, "You better not have gotten me dirty!" and she felt herself to make sure I had not.

"Tomorrow we're going to have a TV, no matter what the cost!" I said. "And I'm not going to stall or change my mind. I'm going to get cable too."

"That would be the best thing you've ever done," she said.

I pressed myself against her. She had her back to me, so she nestled her backside against my body as a sign of gratitude. Then, as if she had suddenly remembered something, she said, "But that doesn't mean I won't be sleeping at my parents' house anymore."

"It's unbelievable how much this girl loves her mother!" I whispered, as if I was talking to myself so she could know my opinion without feeling compelled to respond.

She loved her mother so much, this girl. I mean, I do not know any woman who loves her mother as much. The moment she arrived at her parents' house she would go and kiss her father, and then she would forget all about him, forget he was even in the house. Then she would go straight to her mother and would not leave her side for a second. It was "Mom! Mom!" the entire time. And she would forget all about me, too, as if I were not who I am.

You see, I was the one who was going to buy her a television the next day and sign us up for cable. I was her husband, after all, which was something, especially considering she had just about given up on getting married—not because she was not desirable, but because she was difficult. And well, she was not exactly a paragon of beauty either. Some people might not think she is beautiful at all, plain really. She was almost thirty and had nearly given up on marriage because she wanted to marry above herself. She aimed high, that one! Maybe too high. She had been dreaming of someone better than me, that's for sure. Why? What was so special about her? She said yes to me only because she had gotten tired of looking so high up, and I was suitable. She married me based on a cold mental calculation, but I had no doubt her feelings toward me would grow quickly and deepen. I was five years older, the perfect age difference between a husband and wife—for the wife, of course. More than that would be too much, and less too little.

A while back I told her about my having run into a woman who was in love with me. I told my wife how the woman had blushed with disappointment when I told her I was married. I did not tell my wife how incredibly angry the woman had gotten, though, the time I saw her at the coffee shop and would not talk to her. It was the day after I had gotten her alone—years ago—in my friend's apartment. I thought I would tell my wife about that encounter the next day, after I had bought the twenty-three-inch Sony along with a Berlioz TV cart with wheels, but not about the real reason I would not talk to the woman at the time. I liked to tell my wife these kinds of things so she would understand that getting her had not necessarily been the end of the race for me.

In the morning I asked her to stay at her mother's, and I told her I would call her sometime in the afternoon once I was free and had bought the TV and ordered cable. I also told her that we would be spending the evening at *home*, and she said, "Okay."

I say the word "okay" too, but I pronounce it ok-keh with extra emphasis on the "k" without dragging out the "o" or pronouncing the "y" on the end. She pronounces the "k" without emphasis, drags out the "o," and pronounces the "y" on the end: oh-kayy. The way people who know English pronounce it. I liked that about her. Her English was really good. She could understand everything that was going on in movies even without subtitles. But she was trying to learn French and was always asking me how to say things in French and asking me what certain words mean. Once she wanted to know how to say all the dirty words in French, which really surprised me. She asked me once during a critical moment in bed how to say that while pointing to the *thing* she wanted to know how to say just before it disappeared inside her. I told her I bet it's the same in French as it is in English.

I remember thinking how nice it is to constantly exchange information like that. One day our stores of knowledge would rise to equal levels, like two water containers connected together.

One time she asked me how to say *'ad'id-ni* in French. I told her *'ad* is *mordre*, to bite, but she said, "No. *'Ad'id-ni* doesn't mean 'take a chunk out of my flesh.' It doesn't mean 'gnaw on me.' It means, 'let me feel your teeth on my body.' That's what *'ad'id-ni* means. Hurt me just a little, so I like it." I had not realized the word *'ad'id-ni* meant that. I just thought it was a repetition of *'ad,* to bite. And I had no idea how to say that in French. I had never heard any corresponding French expression, despite having learned all the words having anything to do with sex at a very young age—when I was a young man working as a baggage carrier at the airport . . . No, no, no. I never worked as a baggage carrier at the airport! That was just a slip of the tongue, a *lapsus.*

When I was a student I had a colleague who was going out with a French photojournalist six years older than him. The age difference was not obvious, though, even to us, their closest friends. We were amazed whenever they pointed it out. She knew a little Arabic and was always asking him to teach her Arabic words having to do with sex—until he discovered what he discovered. Their relationship did not last more than a few weeks and almost ended in disaster. She asked me once how to say *remplis-moi* in Arabic. I told her in proper Arabic we would say *imla'-ni,* fill me, from the verb *mala'a-yamla'u,* to fill. "No!" she said. "I want the slang version." So I said we usually say *mallee-ni,* or some people say *tallee-ni,* depending on their educational and social background or what region they are from. "And what about synonyms? Aren't there any other words for it?" I said, "Of course! *'Abbee-ni! Hshee-ni! 'Awwim-ni!*" Her eyes lit up when she heard all those words. Her excitement was not unfamiliar to me, but at the time I did not know where it was coming from. Later on she confessed to me that she had also been seeing a twenty-year-old. My friend and I were twenty-five at the time. The other guy did not know French or English and was illiterate in Arabic. He worked as a baggage carrier at the airport and lived with his family—his father, his pregnant mother, and his five brothers and sisters—in a small apartment that consisted of one big room, a kitchen, a bathroom, and a balcony. (The balcony, actually, was an important part of the story.) She met him by chance one day while photographing the war-torn buildings near where the green line had been in Beirut, near the famous Murr Tower to be exact. He lived in that area. Having gotten lost, she asked him for directions, which he tried to give her, but it took some time since he did not speak a language she understood. He used some English or French words he had picked up at the airport or that he remembered from elementary school and some Arabic words she knew. All the while, she felt irresistibly drawn to him to the point that in a matter of only a few minutes she had become his captive and was ready to give him anything on condition that she could enjoy his body.

While listening to her confessions, I had taken a number of psychological blows, but I did not let on about my suffering to my wife when I was reminded of that event (though I have never really forgotten it for a single day) and told her about it when she asked me to teach her those dirty words in French.

Yes, while listening to the French friend's story I had taken a number of harsh blows, but I had been forced to play the role of a mediator who gave advice standing squarely at equal distance from either of the two. She also revealed to me that what drove her crazy about the other guy was his relationship with his body. "*Il avait un tel rapport à son corps.*" She was bewitched and would say over and over that some kind of magic spell had rattled her brain and twisted her all up inside. I could not stop myself from asking her where she had been meeting with him since she did not have any girlfriends whose apartments she could ask to use. Such women do not even exist in Beirut. A young woman lives either in her parents' or her husband's house, not by herself. She met him at his parents' house where she stayed sometimes for several days (and the nights in between).

"Please don't tell him," she said, meaning my friend. "He's capable of doing something violent. He could hurt himself or me or the guy. Just tell him that every relationship can potentially end at any time. Convince him to leave me alone. I can't live with him like this, with his constant suspicions and jealousy."

I asked her how she managed to be alone with him and have some level of freedom to do things. "At his parents' house," she said. At the end of the night, after everyone went to bed, especially the children, she would go out alone with him on the balcony to a small space no bigger than a square meter. Of course one might expect this to raise some eyebrows, but his mother was really great. She even served them things out on the balcony before going to bed. It was his mother too who invited her to sleep over and stay in the girls' sleeping area. Her boyfriend who was sleeping in the boys' area was the closest person to her with just a narrow walkway separating them, which they occupied after everyone was asleep.

He was afraid of her, though. He thought she was a spy! She tried to convince him that he was all she wanted, nothing more. Maybe she was prepared to be his slave, but a spy? No way. And besides, whom would she be spying on? But he did not trust her and tried to get away from her, even though when he slept with her, it was indescribable. He devoured her.

"You want the truth?" she asked me. "I'm ready to be his slave! Can you believe that?"

I would remain silent and refrain from responding when she said things like this.

That girl blew my mind. She baffled me. I had numerous orgasms just listening to her talk! Such a thing had never happened to me; I did not think it was even possible. I did not even use my hands! This had never happened to me before, and it never happened again, and it was for sure never going to happen in the future. Oh God! What she said turned me on so bad! But as long as she was willing to become that boy's slave, I could never have her. I envied him and wished to be in his place so much that I went to the airport one night hoping to find him, and I think I recognized him since there were not many twenty-year-olds like the boy she had described.

When the news got to my friend, he tried to commit suicide. He took a handful of his mother's sleeping pills, but miraculously he survived. His mother got to him just as he was about to take his last breath. He did not know any details about the young man. All he knew was what his girlfriend had wanted him to know, which was that she was in love with someone else.

Of course I did not tell my wife about the part of the story that shook me up because I had to always look strong in front of her, not like someone with no self-control. I was afraid she would later criticize me every time I looked at another woman in a way she did not like and then accuse me of being weak. Women are by nature much more jealous than men. My wife was not exactly like that, but she was still a woman like any other. A woman is never at rest until her husband has come back to her or she to him. However, my wife did not complain much about these things, especially when she was at her parents' house.

Of course, when I asked her to stay at her parents' house until I got back that day, she did not complain because that was probably what she had been planning to do anyway. In fact, that was exactly what she had been planning to do. My feelings are never wrong about these things. I knew I was asking her to do what she had been planning on doing anyway. But that did not bother me at all, and it certainly did not worry me because these things happen between married people. They happen all the time! Married people just have to deal with them with patience, because if there were not any limits to disagreements, divorce would become the rule, not the exception. Without patience and understanding, it is not possible for a family to enjoy any kind of stability. We would become like the West, where a woman simply bolts out the door without even a "good-bye" the minute she gets frustrated with her husband. It is so true that a person learns many things by being married, things he would not learn any other way. In my own experience, a person is completely different before and after marriage. Marriage teaches you responsibility, and a man who does not know what responsibility is and does not realize its importance in life is missing something.

As I was dozing off on the night that I made my wife a definite promise to buy a television and get cable, I promised myself a good day—a day on which I would win her absolute approval. After buying a TV and getting cable, all she would have to do after coming home was sit back in her chair, press the button, and enjoy whatever shows and movies she liked. It would not occur to her anymore to compare our house to a graveyard (God forbid!) because our house was going to be brightened up with everything she ever wanted and filled with all the sounds she liked. I promised myself that all those efforts I was exerting in order to gain her approval would finally bear fruit and that she would be free of the qualms she still had about me—qualms that seemed to be increasing every day and that made me feel out of control, or, as she had described me, like a car speeding down a hill without any brakes. I hoped she would give herself to me in the evening without any trepidation and make me feel that she was really mine, in action, not just in words or insinuations or silence. I dreamed and fantasized that her change of attitude would be final and absolute and irreversible. I dreamed of the day she would be drenched in sweat as she squirmed with pleasure and devoured every piece of me, wherever she set her lips and whenever she took me into her mouth and swallowed me. I dreamed of devouring her and of her devouring me.

I wished that she would make an effort to please me and that I would become more worthy in her eyes on every level.

I promised myself that her transformation would happen on that particular evening, but before I did anything, I wanted to remove the traces of an unpleasant incident that had occurred between us on our first date, at the Rawda Café, so I bought some beer and put it in my fridge at home. I had made a mistake in the way I treated her then, and she had never asked for a beer ever since.

My wife liked spicy food. She especially liked *samke harrah*, hot and spicy fish. So I ordered it from the best restaurant that specialized in it, which was located at the corniche in 'Ayn Mrayseh. I did not normally worry about meals at home since everything having to do with the kitchen was her duty, but this time I put my customs aside, as well as the beliefs that are connected to my identity—and which I am proud of and do not ever want to change or want anyone else to change, unless fate dictates otherwise.

I wanted to make my wife happy, so I prepared a feast that evening. I wanted her to know how much she meant to me. All day as I worked on the preparations I felt like crying. My feelings stemmed from a deep conviction that if I reconciled with my wife and united with her I would be reconciled with myself. She and I would become one. My desire to cry might have stemmed from the feeling that some of the things I was doing were not a man's duties, which was embarrassing. This was especially the case when I did something no man would do: in my enthusiasm to prove how much she meant to me, I washed her underwear.

I did not literally wash her underwear, but it was almost that. I found her panties and panty hose, which she had left to soak in a small bucket in the bathroom before leaving the house. I rinsed them for her and then wondered how to dry them. I wondered if I should put them on the clothesline on the balcony and let them dry in the sun or hang them inside in the bathroom. I decided to go with the sun! They were the only things hanging on our clothesline, as if on display. When she saw them, she put her hand over her mouth as if trying not to squeal from the shock. She ran and grabbed them from the clothesline and hid them in a drawer. I almost cried because I had always believed that making a gesture to fix things and clear the air between a man and a woman should be a woman's duty, whereas mercy, tenderness, and forgiveness are everyone's duty.

She was shocked when she got back and found all these things waiting for her: the television, cable subscription, and dinner. She had a huge smile on her face.

"Oh my God, I'm so lucky!" she said as she looked at me with gratitude and deep appreciation. In fact, I wanted to reap the benefits of these efforts immediately, so I grabbed the opportunity as she was hugging and kissing me on the mouth to pull her into my arms tightly and carry her to the bed. She submitted to me without any opposition or protest. On the contrary, she was happy. I lay her on the bed and lay down next to her and started caressing her slowly and patiently. I did not rush things; there was no need for rushing since we were at our own house and had the whole day and night. At the same time I was thinking to myself: we could do it now and I could climax once, and then, if possible, I could do the same thing before dinner or when we go to bed. When she saw me taking my time, she got up suddenly, shuddering, and said, "Let me take a shower first." I said, "Why don't you take a shower later? Let's not spoil this beautiful mood." She said, "No! I don't like doing it unless I've just taken a shower."

That excuse she came up with was a total lie. There were many times she enjoyed doing it when she hadn't just taken a shower. On the contrary, she usually got up to take a shower after we were done, most often right after I came. I liked that about her, actually, and still do, because it proved she was not overly experienced in these matters, that she was still pure. The fact that she considered sexual fluids to be dirty was to a certain extent evidence of good morals and purity of heart and lack of experience. But I did not concern myself much about her motives for wanting to shower before doing it because she seemed truthful enough. After all, as she said; she had not showered all day and it had been rather hot and sunny. Maybe she had gone up and down the stairs several times at her mother's since the elevator was broken as usual, never getting properly repaired due to the standing disagreement between the landlord and the tenants. Once she had gotten stuck in the elevator along with some French student. I said to her at the time that she must have been very afraid. "I bet you were scared to death!"

"No," she said. "On the contrary."

"What do you mean on the contrary?"

"I wasn't scared," she said.

"But you always get scared when you get stuck in an elevator," I said.

"I get scared just like everybody else."

What I gathered from this exchange was that she had not been afraid when the elevator got stuck with the French guy in there with her. I never supposed for a second that the French guy had been there because he was accompanying her or that they were in some sort of a relationship. At any rate, he had not lived there for some time, and there was no longer any opportunity for the elevator to break down with her in it, all alone with him, unafraid.

She came out of the shower and said, "What do you say we eat now? I just can't wait to taste that delicious dinner of yours."

"Why not?" I said. "Let's eat!"

The food was excellent. She loved it and thanked me for preparing it. She said she really was not expecting anything like that, nor was she expecting me to rinse the underwear she had left to soak. That last part she did not actually mention, as if she had forgotten all about it. That was another sign of decency and nobility on her part.

Unfortunately, though, my joy that night was not complete because the cable people did not come to hook up the TV and install the other components and program the channels. They told me, "Tomorrow," even though I tried to bribe them with more money. They just could not do it. I told her that tomorrow our happiness would be complete, and she said it was no problem. "We can wait one more day!" I appreciated her understanding and was comforted by her laid-back nature. But as soon as she was done with her dinner, she said she was tired. I suggested we go to bed after we clear the table since I was tired too from running around all day. Without answering, she went directly to the bedroom, plopped herself down on the bed—on her stomach—as if she was so exhausted she could not even hold herself up. She shut her eyes and stopped talking and moving as if she had fallen immediately to sleep. She would not answer me unless I prodded her, and then all she spoke was gibberish. Then as I was caressing her she fell asleep for real. I continued to caress her while she slept. I felt the warmth of her body and its suppleness at my touch, which made me think she felt totally safe and secure and had fallen into a rare and delightful slumber. That was what drove me to continue with more fervor, more tenderness, and more attention. When she became like pliant dough in my hands, I moved aside only the parts of her clothing that were in my way and went inside her without putting my weight on her so as not to interrupt the rhythm of her breathing. It was a moment in my life unlike any other. She received me into her slumber as if it had been for my sake, just for me. In that rare state of bliss, I ejaculated quickly, but I pulled out of her at the right moment and did not come inside her.

I usually did not come inside her anyway for reasons that I never revealed to her. I wanted a boy, not a girl, and to conceive a boy there is a certain way to have sex. A certain way to ejaculate, actually. For a woman to conceive a boy, she has to be in a specific position. But this time there was another reason I did not do it, which had nothing at all to do with her getting pregnant since she was already pregnant at the time and the method of conception did not matter anymore. In all honesty, I came on her because I wanted to. Just like that. She started squirming after a little while, after my fluid got cold on her skin, but I hurried to wipe it off with a towel I had wet with warm water. After I finished, and after she felt me getting up to do something else, she said, "You better not have gotten my clothes dirty or the sheets either!"

"No," I said. "Don't worry. It all landed on you."

"Where on me?" she snapped. "You think I'm a sidewalk?"

"No. It was all on your back and bottom," I said.

"Are you sure?"

"Yeah!"

"Did you wipe it all up?"

"Yeah!"

I think she was worried some of it got on her hair down there, which would mean she would have to get up and wash. After that she went back to sleep.

That last thing she said, which was a complaint of sorts, wasn't out of bad intentions at all, and it was certainly not a rejection of me. Evidence of that was when I was trying to go inside her while she was sleeping, I missed at first. She felt that I missed and helped me out with some sleepy movements from her backside until everything was lined up just right. And she welcomed me in, being all wet and slippery in the spot where I entered, not dry and tight and difficult like it usually was. It was like a frothy, toothless mouth. That was clear proof that I had begun to be, or maybe already was, something wonderful in her mind. It was obvious. Anybody who did not squeeze his eyes shut could see that.

That night I slept like a baby. I felt things between us were going to be all right, that everything would work out. She was in my bed in every meaning of the word. She was near me. She was mine.

When the cable people came at around ten the next morning, my wife was getting ready to go to her mother's. She was going to help her shop for underwear. She always spent the day with her mother under some pretense or another. Lately, the excuse was underwear. She never got very specific about what kind of underwear exactly, but I knew what she meant. The baby was on the way, and it was already time to start taking care of him. That was why I always let her go without asking questions that would upset her. I decided a while back to just let her go to her mother's without making a big fuss every time.

After about an hour and a half, the TV was beaming eighty stations—some satellite, some cable, local and international—into our living room. The technician fine-tuned them one at a time, showing each one to me proudly, like someone accustomed to inspiring awe. He described each channel to me, going on in great detail about a few stations in particular that showed "bold" movies late at night. "What if there are children in the house?" I inquired.

"We can block them at the customer's request."

When he finished checking all the stations and everything was in good working order, he gave me the remote and I placed it on the table in front of the couch where my wife always sat. I told myself I would not touch it until she came home and broke it in with her own beautiful hands. That is how I am. I like for a woman to be the first person to break in anything new of mine. It gives me shivers and makes me feel secure. After that, I left the house.

I came back home between two and three o'clock after having lunch with the "Thursday group." A long time ago, long before I got married, a number of friends and I from the various sects that make up the larger Lebanese family got into this habit: we would eat *mulukhiyyeh* the first Thursday of every month at the Blue Note, a restaurant that, like many of the restaurants in Beirut scattered around AUB, served *mulukhiyyeh* as its daily special on those days. There were five of us. Four of us were drinking, including myself. We were drinking red Lebanese wine at a time when Lebanon was still in the never-ending transitional phase into good times after a very long and destructive war. A lot of people felt a yearning for peace and a special affection for their wounded country. The wine was good, so I drank. The lunch provided a nice occasion to praise the homeland. Lebanon, the land of diversity and tolerance: there we sat at one table, as friends, raising our glasses (filled with wine or water, it didn't matter), drinking to people we loved and remembered. "This country must remain forever. To Lebanon! The diverse, the tolerant. To Lebanon, the land of public and personal liberties; Lebanon, the land of the free press. To Lebanon, where women enjoy more freedom than anywhere else in the entire region and participate fully in the media revolution, in television and in radio, etcetera, etcetera."

Sometime between two and three o'clock I was on my way home. On the sidewalk out in front of the entrance to my building, I ran into her—the seamstress who had made us some curtains a month before.

I was on my way home from that lunch, having had too much to eat and drink. I was about to fall asleep with a raging desire—for my wife, who was not coming back before dark. That would not be for another three or four hours. How I wished she were there, even if she would not be in the same mood that I was in. I would have been persistent like I usually was when I wanted her and she was not in the mood, and she would have taken care of the situation in her own way. She never ran out of tricks and exit plans.

At that time, I did not know the seamstress's name, and I do not think my wife knew it either. We had not asked her name when we went to her place. We had been looking for a seamstress to sew us some curtains for our bedroom in the apartment we rented after we got married. The neighbors had referred us to her, so we went to the house where she and her family lived. She was unmarried and still is. She was around the same age as my wife. She had agreed to our offer, and we decided that she would come to our house the next day to take some measurements and sort out any other details.

When she found out that we were newlyweds and that it had only been a few days since we were married, she blushed in a way that was concerning. It was not the kind of blushing associated with shyness. The way she would look at my wife, it was as if she were trying to figure out what she must have been like before our marriage. Her eyes flitted like a scanner or a copier, to borrow my wife's expression. It was as if she were constantly comparing the image in front of her to an image of my wife that she had drawn in her mind.

The seamstress looked at my wife with fascination; she blushed. Her nose glistened with sweat, and she shielded herself from our stares by pulling her scarf down her forehead as far as possible and lowering her head.

"Truth be told, every time she looks at us it's like our eyes are a camera flash about to go off," my wife said.

"She's like a child trying to avoid her parents' scolding," I said.

Her anxiety may have been a result of the jealousy that burned inside her. Perhaps she was jealous of my wife and wanted to be in her place. She asked us who had referred us to her, and we said it was a neighbor. "Which neighbor?" she asked. "What's his name?" When I told her it was the grocer, she looked around making sure no one was there but us. Then she said, "Was it the one at the corner or the one in the middle of the street?" I said the one at the corner, and she became silent. She remained silent as if she had decided to handle things her own way.

I wanted to tell her that many people had recommended her and not just the grocer at the corner. However, I kept quiet as well even though I wanted to say something from the bottom of my heart. The grocer at the corner was unmarried—I found out afterwards. She was no doubt shaken by the fact that my wife and I were newlyweds, that we could enjoy each other as we pleased—wherever, whenever, in any way and as much as we wanted, in seriousness and in jest, in cleanliness and in laziness, in slumber and in wakefulness, naked or fully dressed—whereas she was unmarried and dying of a desire that could not be consummated. For between a man and a woman are myriad things God has forbidden except in marriage! Marriage is the rightful means through which mountains are removed off the chests of young women, the means through which hearts and minds are put to rest.

Then the seamstress bluntly asked us a question that would not normally come to anyone's mind. She asked us if we had gotten married out of love or "tedium," so I asked her, "What do you mean by tedium?" She said that for many people, marriage happens as a result of one person thinking, "Oh God! Oh God! Let me just get this thing over and done with once and for all." She said that perhaps we had gotten married because our parents kept nagging us, especially my wife's parents. Or that perhaps we had gotten married because we were sick and tired of the whole thing and just succumbed to the desires of those around us. "*That* is tedium," she said. I was shaken because I had never thought about it that way. Suddenly, I felt as if this woman was stripping me naked. Was I too one of those people who had gotten married out of "tedium"?

My first meeting with my wife had been arranged with marriage in mind. I had not known her beforehand. The first time I heard of her was through my aunt, who for a while had been more concerned about my marital status than my own mother. No doubt my aunt had also been concerned about my mother herself. My bachelorhood had been taking its toll on my mother's nerves because she was constantly worrying about me: How would I survive without her if—God forbid—she got hurt or died? After all, most of my siblings were abroad either in the Gulf or Australia, and those who were still in Beirut were busy with their own families.

Out of the blue, my aunt said to me one day, "Let me introduce you to our neighbors' daughter who lives in the building across from us. She's gorgeous!"

It was strange, that feeling of nakedness that the seamstress's comments about "tedium" had invoked in me. It felt strange because I am not one of those ultrasensitive people who can't sleep at night until the last plane has landed safely in every last airport on the planet. Not at all! I sleep soundly because I know that with or without me life will go on as it always has. So why had I been so shaken up by her remark that perhaps I had gotten married "out of tedium," or "just because people get married"? Why should people get married "for" a reason anyway? It was when people started marrying for love that the divorce rate went up! And despite that—I mean despite the bluntness that this woman had shown—there was some sort of a cry for help in her eyes that had caught my attention. It was like a light that flashed intermittently. When I ran into her on the street, I wondered why her parents allowed her to leave the house with that light, that cry for help, lurking in her eyes. I thought her father and brothers must hit her constantly because she was always letting on about things that should remain hidden, which made me sad. It made me so sad I kept wondering how I could possibly help her! I would console myself by saying that surely nobody else could see what I had seen in her eyes. But then again, I never saw her alone. A woman younger than her, who appeared to be twenty years old or so, always accompanied her. That was probably upon her family's insistence because they knew her well and worried about her. That realization removed my feelings of consolation and allowed my feelings of pity to resurface.

However, she was alone that time I ran into her at the entrance of the building after coming back from my lunch. I approached her right away without prior planning or premeditation, but rather automatically like someone who had been programmed to do that. I don't say "programmed" to justify what I did but because that's what it was. Sometimes a person rushes into things because he's afraid of thinking about consequences, which might cause him to hesitate.

That wasn't my case, however. I didn't rush in because I was afraid of changing my mind. Actually, I think the word "programmed" is the perfect way to describe the situation. Seeing her was like clicking a computer mouse and causing the system to start immediately. Just like that, I went up to her and told her that the curtains needed fixing.

Without looking at me, she said bluntly, "They couldn't possibly need fixing yet! It's too soon."

"They do," I said and kept walking as I beckoned her with a nod to follow me, which she did. She walked a few steps behind me.

I opened the door and went in, but she just stood at the door. "Come in," I said, and when she didn't move or say anything, I pulled her inside. After I shut the door behind her she asked me if my wife was home, but I didn't respond. I took her in my arms and started kissing her and caressing her body. She neither surrendered nor protested, but she was nervous. Of course, she was enjoying it—until I slipped my hand down her belly and between her thighs. That's when she started panting and inhaling and exhaling like a wild animal that had stepped into a trap. A few seconds later, she transformed into a lamb in my arms, a very heavy lamb! When she was about to fall down, I lay her on the couch. She was unconscious but alive. She was breathing, but she couldn't talk, except to let out some periodic moans. The only frightening thing about her was the way her eyes rolled into the back of her head. I closed her mouth shut as soon as I lay her on the couch, thinking it would increase her sense of pleasure and help her get through this stage— the stage of ecstasy at the peak of orgasm. But her mouth seemed like a separate entity, dissociated from things I could maneuver. I should have realized immediately that the girl had fainted and that I was in trouble and should get out of that situation immediately before it got worse and the repercussions escalated. But my medical knowledge is quite limited, and the girl had not passed out due to common reasons like cold or illness or things of that nature that could be treated with something as simple as a sip of rose water or a cup of tea. I wandered through the house from one room to another as if the solution was to just wander around. After a few minutes had passed with her still in that condition, I decided to contact her family. Since I didn't know their number or if they even had a phone in the first place, I decided to go to them directly and tell them what happened so I could relieve myself of any responsibility. After all, they were her family and they surely knew more about her condition. I decided I would just pretend that she had come to fix the curtains and that she had fallen weak all of a sudden when she got to the top of the ladder but managed to bear the discomfort until she reached the couch. I decided I must tell them that she reached the couch and lay down by herself. I couldn't embarrass them by telling them that I had carried her the whole distance from the ladder to the couch, which was a few meters. It would not be easy for the family, especially the brothers, to accept that a stranger had held their sister all that distance even if she had been unconscious. I would tell them that my wife left after their daughter had asked her to go get something she needed for the curtains.

I was sure that my wife would not get home until long after everybody had left the house and everything had returned to normal. But she arrived shortly after they did, no more than a minute or two. She came in yelling and demanding an explanation. "What's going on? What's going on?" Of course the last thing she could have anticipated was to see her husband accused of rape! Her husband who never tired of telling her how much he loved her and how, with every day that passed, his love for her was growing in his heart.

"I love you." I said that about ten times a day. I said it so many times that she once told me, "Lucky you! How easy it must be for you to say that." That day, I liked what she said because it seemed to me as if she had this desire to proclaim her love to me as well but couldn't fulfill that desire because she wasn't used to it and because she was too shy to do it because of her conservative upbringing.

Every day I would leave her a note to find in one of the containers she used in the morning, like the coffee or sugar canister. Each time, I wrote a new, beautiful message expressing my love for her. Sometimes I'd find my notes forgotten on the kitchen table or the stove. Deep down, I wished she would save them somewhere safe along with all her other valuables. I'm sure reading them made her happy because when I asked her the first time how she felt about these notes, she blushed and asked me where I had learned to do that. I learned it from an article I read about a leftist Lebanese thinker who, according to the article, had been assassinated by "the dark forces." He loved his wife so much that he wrote her a note every day that ended with an exclamation mark—a note that he put in a container that she was going to use. The bizarre thing about that article was that his wife did not believe him. She actually accused him of having affairs with other women. Among the messages that were quoted in the article were "The sea is forever committed to its shores! The sea is forever blissful with its shores!" and, on March 21, the first day of spring, "Spring suits you!"

Lots of people came: the seamstress's father, two brothers, a sister, and the young cousin I always saw with her. They didn't all show up at once, but a few at a time. Each group would come in all upset and leave the door wide open, not out of carelessness, but on purpose, because they knew others would be coming after them and because they knew they wouldn't be staying more than a few moments—the amount of time it would take to pick her up and get her out of there. But in those very moments, their daughter began regaining consciousness. The last to arrive was her oldest brother, who came in a few seconds after my wife arrived. I had never met him before, not even when my wife and I went to her place about the curtains. I looked right at him as he came for me and began throwing punches the moment he got close enough. He had taken me by surprise, and that enabled him to knock me to the floor, get on top of me, and keep hitting me as hard as he wanted. He surprised me because when I expected him to attack me from the east, he attacked me from the west, and when I expected him from the west, he attacked from the east. It was impossible for me not to be taken by surprise. It was an all-out assault. Who doesn't get surprised by an assault? I started screaming at him, calling him crazy so my wife would hear. My wife had been surrounded by all those women and men who had rallied around her to inform her about that evil husband of hers who had defiled this delicate young girl's innocence and honor and her family's honor, this poor young girl who had fragile nerves, which was an honorable condition that anyone might suffer from. What noble person these days, in these vicious times, didn't suffer from frayed nerves? Her brother had me in a tight hold and was taking out his frustrations on me until he noticed the presence of my wife and quickly left me and went after her. He grabbed her right in front of everyone, lifted her dress, and grabbed hold of her crotch over her panties. "This right here," he screamed for everyone to hear, "This is the cunt of a whore . . . !"

Oh my God!

My wife was screaming in pain; streams and streams of tears poured down her cheeks. Without a thought I pounced on him to avenge her and free her from his offensive, dirty hands, but he was faster than me and dropped me to the floor once again. He was like a bull, a raging bull.

After everyone left (he was the last to leave, saying, "You'll pay for this!" on his way out), I realized I was all alone in the house. My wife was nowhere to be found. She was not in any of the rooms or in the bathroom or on the balcony or under the bed or even under the couch. She must have left with them or immediately after them. So I waited.

I waited long enough for her to get to her mother's and then I called. Her mother said, "No, she's not here!" Her answer was disconcertingly harsh, as if she wanted to scold me for calling, as if I didn't have the right to call my wife if we had a disagreement or faced some kind of difficulty. Suddenly my wife's cell phone—which she had never left behind since the day she bought it, long before we got married—started ringing. It had been tossed onto the couch. What the hell! Could she possibly still be here somewhere even though I hadn't seen her when I searched every corner of the house? The phone kept ringing, though, without her coming to answer it, so I was forced to answer. It was her mother! Having suddenly gotten very worried when she heard my voice on her daughter's cell phone, she said, "Where's my daughter?"

I didn't know what to say. After some hesitation I said, "She must have gone to the store to buy something and will be right back because she left her phone here."

"I'm sure she forgot it," she said. Then after a few moments of silence she said in a panicky voice, "Turn it off until she gets back!"

I didn't say yes and I didn't say no! I just hung up without saying good-bye or anything so she would know I was upset by what she said. Did she have the right to meddle in such matters just because she was her mother? I didn't turn off my wife's phone. But that wasn't because I was trying to find out what secrets my wife was keeping from me. I never thought that she was keeping big secrets from me. I was sure that if she were hiding anything from me it would be the kind of harmless stories women share among themselves. Less than fifteen minutes later, her phone line was completely cut off. She must have called the company to request they cancel the service, claiming that she lost her phone!

That was clear!

I mean her position was clear; she wanted to escalate things.

Yes. But that didn't necessarily mean she was getting calls from people who should remain unknown to me, people with whom she had inappropriate relations.

I tried calling several times after that, but it was always her mother, who answered the same way, "She's not here!"

But where could she be so late in the evening if not there?

"She is there!" I said to her mother. It wasn't as if she had a habit of sleeping away from home after all. She finally told me she was there but she didn't want to talk to me. "Fine," I said.

I said to myself that my wife should not distract me from what was happening on the other end with the seamstress's family. I told myself that the key to the whole problem was there, with the single shopkeeper she asked us about after everyone left and we were all alone. It was not going to be easy for me to go out into the streets so soon, with the event still fresh and undoubtedly the talk of the town, especially since these days there wasn't much for people to talk about. The Gulf War was over; the bombing of Iraq was over along with images of the Iraqi Army ending up as corpses in the deserts or lost soldiers wandering aimlessly. The Lebanese war was over too. There were no crises in the world now to occupy people, like the massacres in Bosnia and Herzegovina and Kosovo, or the destruction of Chechnya, or the targeting of Osama Bin Laden in Afghanistan with a satellite-guided missile or two from an American warship in the middle of the Pacific Ocean, nor the famous handshake between Arafat and Rabin in Washington. And Israel had not bombed the power stations that day, either, causing the electricity to go out in Beirut for entire months . . . Nothing like that happened on that afternoon whose name and date I, the interested party, have forgotten. Nothing happened that might have distracted people from my incident, so how could I go out? Despite that, however, I went out. That was my way of expressing my innocence loudly and clearly. I spoke to the shopkeeper who was at least ten years my elder, meaning he was about fifteen years older than the seamstress, and I asked him to be frank with me. I told him I would be frank with him too.

"You shouldn't have done what you did!" he said.

"What did I do?" I asked.

"You tried to take advantage of an innocent girl who trusted you. She went up to your place on the assumption that you were married and that your wife was at home."

"That's true!"

"But your wife was not at home. Wasn't it shameful to take her that way the moment she stepped across the threshold, the stench of wine clearly on your breath? That is shameful, there's nothing else to call it! I know exactly what happened. Don't you dare do it ever again!"

I asked him if she was related to him, and he said no. But he said he had lived in this neighborhood before that girl had even been born and knew her very well. She was a good girl, very polite, but whenever she became emotional she would faint. Then he advised me to watch out for her brothers because there was nothing they weren't capable of doing. They were shameless. Usually people like them who have had such a thing happen to them either take matters into their own hands or just try to hide it; these guys were out to rob people. As far as they were concerned, money was the solution to everything. "If you don't give them what they want, you better watch out because they might take you to court. They have lots of witnesses, among them one in particular whose testimony cannot be refuted: your wife! And the way I see it, you cannot take them to court for doing what they did to your wife, in spite of any allegation that you may have, and I don't think I'm wrong in my opinion. You saw without any doubt where her brother grabbed your wife and how he squeezed her hard enough to make her cry more from the shame than the pain itself, and you yourself were surprised by the flood of tears down her face. Your wife will not be happy about you raising a case over it even if you wanted to, and you can't raise a case on her behalf without her consent. You are in a predicament that can only be solved with money!"

Oh my God! How did he know all these details? Where else could he have gotten them except from the seamstress? No question. They obviously had a solid, long-lasting relationship.

"Step in," I told him.

"No way," he said. "I can't get in the middle of this and try to play mediator. We have an old and deep-rooted enmity between us . . . over her!"

He was not willing to divulge in what way "over her" or anything else.

He advised me to call them right away and make them an offer, say five hundred dollars, and let the page be turned immediately—and the whole thing be forgotten for good.

"Are you sure?"

He could not confirm it one hundred percent, but he advised me to do it anyway. Who could guarantee anything one hundred percent? They might ask for more money or something, but in his opinion, this path would no doubt lead to a solution.

Later that evening—which I spent thinking about the shopkeeper's advice without reaching a decision—instead of calling the seamstress's brothers, I called my wife on her parents' landline in a final attempt to talk to her. She answered the phone after the first ring, which I was expecting. I expected her to be sitting in front of the television, watching one of those movies whose heroines she liked to emulate, the phone next to her at arm's length, ready to grab it as soon as it rang to avoid waking up her parents because she knew I would call. She didn't say much, despite my persistence. She succinctly said that she was not coming back home, period. I responded confidently, "Even better." Among the things she said was "I will not spend my time waiting on you while you do time in prison for trying to rape the neighbors' sick daughter!"

"What the hell are you talking about?" I said. "What rape? What sick daughter? You know her as well as I do, if not better. What prison are you talking about?" Before I retaliated with my "even

better" response, I tried explaining to her that I was innocent of all
the things they had tried to get her to believe about me. I told her
that I did not do anything! I told her it was the girl who suddenly felt
sick while she was at the top of the ladder, examining the curtains.
As for the curtains, I told her they were missing several rings. I said
that I ran into the seamstress by chance on my way back home and
told her about the missing rings, but that I didn't think for one
minute that she would come up to the house right away. However,
my wife did not want to listen and was convinced of the information
she had received. In fact, she was convinced of whatever she wanted
to believe because it suited her own interests. She was convinced she
was right about her decision not to come back home. When I asked
her, "Aren't you coming back tonight?" she replied, "Not tonight,
not tomorrow night. Never!" That's when I said, "Even better,"
with utmost confidence.

That night, as I sat alone in my apartment in the late evening,
or rather early night, I had no choice but to break in my new
television myself, in my wife's absence. Why would I wait when
she might not be coming back for a few more days or a week or
even more? She was stubborn by nature and would no doubt try to
impose some new conditions on me, the way she did every time we
had a disagreement, even if it was over something petty. She always
blew things out of proportion and never backed down until she had
scored a new victory. At any rate, it was not the first time she had left
the house. I was sure she would come back even though I knew that
this time was different from the other times.

"I'll never go anywhere near that neighborhood again," she
had yelled at me on the phone. "I couldn't face her or any of
her brothers!"

Still, I was sure she was coming back because I hadn't revealed
my hand to her. I hadn't flashed my cards in her mother's face or
in front of other people. I didn't make her mother hide her face in
shame over her daughter's behavior, her daughter whom she always
defended. As soon as I did, however, she would come back, small
and humiliated, and occupy a tiny corner of the house. But I did
not want her to come back that way. I wanted her to come back
with dignity. She was my wife after all! She wouldn't be gone for a

long time. She was coming back. It might be a few days, but she was coming back.

Of course I thought about sticking to my first wish, which was to wait and let her break in our new television, but I knew I couldn't bear waiting like that for several days, all by myself, while she did as she pleased at her parents' house. So, in a moment of anger, I grabbed the remote control, turned on the TV, and started browsing through the different channels, acquainting myself with them, without the slightest feeling of guilt.

Oh my God!

There were dozens of channels from all over the world: eighty channels in all the earth's languages and colorful dialects, an array of lighting and design, innumerable variations in human form, and movies. Almost all of the movies on the various channels, however, were in English. Some were translated and others dubbed, and some were just in English with no subtitles at all. It was truly incredible. I was frustrated because I did not know English. I felt like I was missing out on so many things. A flood of news, films, and shows was gushing out before my eyes, but I could not really benefit from it. I felt slighted. It seemed knowing English had become a prerequisite for justice these days.

I did not know how much time had passed as I browsed through different channels, noting their names and programming them as I pleased, before I stumbled upon a movie that jolted me like an electric shock. It was a porn movie! Was my wife watching it? That was the first thought that came to my mind. I wanted to call and ask her immediately. If only she had not forgotten her cell phone here, she wouldn't have canceled her service and gotten a new number, and I would have been able to reach her. There was no way I could call her at this late hour on her parents' landline. All sorts of thoughts went through my mind as those scenes opened up before me with no end in sight. My thoughts went so far as to wonder whether my wife was at her sleeping parents' house watching the movie alone or with someone else because I knew that she was in the habit of having friends over late at night after her parents were sound asleep. She had let me in one time, very quietly, so we would not wake her parents. "Sit down over here," she had commanded. She sat me in a corner of the living room where she knew her parents never went, and she sat down beside me. We sat there intimately, glued to each other for a long time, my hand roaming freely and quietly as we watched a rather risqué movie. Before leaving, I told her it was the first time in my life I had done anything like that—staying up that late at a woman's house and doing such things while her parents were sleeping. I was expecting her to tell me it was her first time as well, but she didn't say anything, as if she hadn't been listening to what I said.

Those television scenes still fill me with mixed feelings of shock, repulsion, arousal, and fear. Maybe I fear that someone might catch me by surprise. I also feel nervous—maybe I am nervous that those people who are not ashamed of doing all those things in front of me might notice that I am—that someone is— watching them. Then, like a stunning blow, I caught the gaze that the woman in the movie cast toward me while she held onto her partner's penis as if it were the cross of salvation or some rare prize for which blood must be shed. Like a stunning blow, I caught her gaze toward me, toward the camera. She looked at me with such oppressive vulgarity, ruining my feelings of desire and fulfillment and intimacy. It was as if she had caught me looking at her so attentively and decided to mock me. Her look said, "I saw you too." It was as if she told me with that look of hers that she was not doing these things in secrecy and knew that the camera was transporting her into the homes of others. I felt that others were watching me too, and I was flustered and burned with jealousy when the camera zoomed in on the man's penis as his girlfriend held it in her hands, flaunting it as if it were some dazzling pagan statue. I burned with jealousy because I remembered something that my wife had once said before we got married. It was sunset and we were taking a walk along the seaside Manarah Boulevard. The sun looked like a huge disc of fire on the verge of touching the sea, so we stopped to watch and enjoy the view. I was carried away as I contemplated the view, relishing every moment and thinking of the beauty of this world. I found the scene both stunning and gentle at the same time. In the meantime, my wife stood there smiling as she tried to keep herself from laughing. "Look at this beautiful scene," I said. "The sun looks like a huge disc of fire sinking into the sea. I

wonder what will happen when this burning body of fire touches the
water. Will vapor rise and fill the horizon?" She burst out laughing
for no apparent reason. Before I had a chance to ask her why she
was laughing, she said the view reminded her of something she had
heard. Some man had compared the shape of the sun at sunset to
his erection! He had said, "Look! The sun looks like the head of my
cock!" Where had she heard that kind of talk? What kind of people
had she been associating with?

"What did you just say?" I asked her. I could not believe my
ears. I had been expecting her to be moved by my tender and poetic
description. I was even talking to her in a low voice, suitable for that
charming view. She said it was something her friend's boyfriend
had said. He was mad at his girlfriend, and when she said, "Don't
you just love the sunset? See the sun? It looks like—," he didn't
even let her finish her sentence. "Like the head of my cock," he had
responded, completing her sentence.

My fiancée—the woman who was soon to be my wife—burst into
a fit of hysterical laughter. When I heard those words come out of
her mouth and watched her laugh uncontrollably, my eyes popped in
amazement. Some poor people who could not afford to get out of the
city in the summer started descending onto the corniche in droves
now that the sun was setting and the heat of the day was beginning to
wane. What was so funny about this vulgar analogy? It was the kind of
thing, in my experience anyway, that men—a certain class of men—
might laugh about amongst themselves. When she saw me flustered
like that, she took my hand and said, "I am so happy, my dear
husband, that you are SO polite. I love you!" She was embarrassed
and regretful about what she had said. It was a refreshing indication
that she was heading in the right direction; I needed to be patient.
That was what the situation required. It was marriage, after all, which
spanned a lifetime and children and destiny. I had to gently let her
discover her mistakes every time on her own, without crushing her.

I liked it when she called me her husband even though we were
not married yet, and I used to dream of the day she would tell me
she wanted to have my child. In fact, I expected her to say that
before we got married, or afterwards, but definitely before she got
pregnant. I was also hoping and waiting to hear her say the word

"pregnant" in English—the way she usually did when mentioning things she was bashful about. It was a word I learned from her because she always used it instead of the Arabic word. But the nice effect that her calling me her husband had on me did not stop me from thinking about the shock I felt from that bizarre analogy. Was it true that her friend's boyfriend had made the comment? Or did she concoct the part about her friend's boyfriend when in fact she was the one who had seen the resemblance—between the sun setting into the sea, on the shores of Beirut, and the head of a man's cock all red and swollen with arousal? How had she come up with that? People only make comparisons between things they know, things they have experienced.

These scenes were still unfolding before me, still had a grip on me, rousing such desire in me as I had never felt before. Once my wife told me that porn films were like chemical fertilizers; they make the fruits and vegetables grow faster and bigger, but make them lose the most important thing—their flavor! How did my wife know that . . . my wife, who, whenever she saw me looking bewildered by her words or could read all sorts of questions and suspicions in my eyes, always said she had read it in some English-language magazine?

Then my body went limp. I felt as though exhaustion had overpowered me. I pulled a few tissues out of the Kleenex box, and out came one of those promotional prizes the manufacturers put in to market their products. I wiped myself off and before falling asleep on the couch, I wished I could cover up that machine there in front of me—the TV that is—with something thick, like steel maybe, something that could stop all that sleazy stuff inside it from creeping into my living room. Oh God! This was the atomic bomb people used to talk about. Was it going to explode? Had my father been so afraid of it that he put off letting us get one as long as possible? Was that why he had been so strict about limiting the amount of time we spent sitting in front of it when we finally did get one? He was always complaining that the TV gave him chest pains and made him feel overwhelmed and in a bad mood; it also made him worry about us kids. We weren't alone in our own home anymore, he would say. We weren't complete human beings anymore—we had been reduced to a heap of glazed eyes and perked ears.

I went to bed very disturbed by what I had watched. That movie alone was enough to shake a mountain, let alone the dozens of other channels that roared like a waterfall inside that hellbox all day long. I was not going to call the seamstress's brother in the morning, and I was not going to let them rob me either. I was not going to pay them one lira for their silence. I would leave my house the next day very normally, as if nothing had happened, because nothing had happened.

I was expecting my aunt to call to ask me a question or tell me something or check to see how I was doing at least, but she never called. I would call her and tell her that if she had heard about it not to tell my mother. I did not want my mother to find out before the details of the situation had been sorted out. It would be embarrassing for her to see her son beaten down and in such a weak and powerless position. She would be devastated. As long as it was still possible to mend matters, there was no point in revealing my weakened position with respect to my wife in my mother's eyes and no point making her deal with the shock and fret over it. I did not want anyone to know.

Could my mother still not know yet?

At the outset of the first day after my wife left me, I told myself it was just a head-butting stage and we were still at the beginning. I had to be very crafty and extremely cautious. I could not forget that I had not committed any sin, had not done anything for which I should be punished. I had to maintain that position, which was the truth! I had to act as if everything that happened had been part of some big plan, like a trap, as though it was exactly what my wife had wanted, like a self-fulfilling wish. That's right. She had her excuse for now, but despite everything, I was confident she would come back.

She would come back tomorrow, if not today.

I did not call any of my friends that entire day. I turned the answering machine on so I could answer only the calls I wanted to answer. I definitely did not want to answer a call from the seamstress's brother, who called twice and left a message stating nothing but his name. I also did not want to answer a call from any of my relatives or friends who might ask me about my wife because that would not be an easy topic to discuss. It would expose me,

expose my domestic situation, that is, and the fact that matters were
out of my control. One thing I would not put up with was people
saying that my wife walked out the door whenever she pleased as if
I wasn't there. Neither would I allow people to say I didn't "satisfy"
her or "provide" her with everything her heart desired. Rumor had
it among my buddies that a wife whose husband "satisfied" her—
sexually, of course—and "provided" everything she needed couldn't
possibly object to anything. It killed me to remember what one of
my friends was always saying, that so-and-so was "sleeping" with so-
and-so because her husband always fell asleep the moment his head
hit the pillow at night. I spent every night wide-awake trying to pull
my wife close to me, by trickery most of the time and sometimes by
force. If my friends' theory was correct, then I should have been
the one running around with other women because the second my
wife's head hit the pillow she would pass out! "My wife *howls* when
I go inside her," one of my buddies said once, with the intention
of letting us know he was so manly no woman could stand it and he
should be envied for it and his wife would never leave him or shut
the door behind her without saying, "See you later," because she
could never find another man as well endowed. Women talk, you
know. He should get a medal for it.

I didn't call any of my friends that entire day, which I spent
at home alone watching TV—that marvelous world. My father was
exactly right about one thing—that at the very least the television
debilitated a person with all its dangerous and bewitching magic.
As I watched all those scenes and enchanting women, all those
programs, all the animals and the forests, I almost forgot about
my problems with the seamstress and my wife. I watched a program
about a woman who gave birth to a baby girl out on the limb of a
tree that dozens of people were clinging to as they tried to escape a
flood that had engulfed their area. A helicopter arrived with a crew
of white people. They got the woman and her newborn out first and
then saved the others. I was surprised with myself for hoping some
of the rescuers were Lebanese because, according to the news we
got in Lebanon, our reputation there in Africa was generally not
very good. And I watched a rerun of the first moon landing and
then some animals having sexual intercourse, and I won't deny I

got a little turned on. I watched fashion models for hours on end. Models, models, models. Clothes, clothes, clothes. I saw everything from overcoats that covered every part of the body to bathing suits that hid nothing but what the censors would block out and clothes that covered things only to make them more revealing. And I saw a movie, German I think, in which two girls that had to be under twenty years old kissed each other very passionately! I also watched a soccer game between two teams from Ecuador that I never dreamed I'd be able to see. My wife had told me once that Madonna—the famous singer and sex symbol—was infatuated with the goalie on the Italian soccer team and was wild with desire to meet him. I also saw a tennis match, a basketball game, the Great Wall of China, magicians and jugglers, and circus performers with some very slender and enticing females among them. What didn't I see that day!

I'm a hundred percent sure that if my wife had been watching TV, she would not have gotten up from the couch until long after completely forgetting she even had a husband. Indeed, long after forgetting I'd ever been born and planted my two feet on the face of this earth. It is the devil itself, I tell you! The TV, that is.

I did not contact anybody that day. But I did call her—my wife—in the evening. Her mom answered the phone and said she was not there. I said thank you and hung up. It was that simple. Her mother's answer—which feigned ignorance and innocence and which revealed her stance as someone who would not get involved and help us to reconcile—infuriated me. She did not ask me about anything, and she did not seem worried at all about her daughter's fate. After I hung up on her, I said to myself, "I am not worried either. What's the worst that could happen?" and I stretched out in front of the TV. (Thank God I had bought the TV. What else would I have done all day?) I started browsing through the channels, hoping I would stumble upon a nice movie or show, or anything really, so I could spend the night watching it. I was anxious I might come across a movie like last night's, but I did not. I kept searching but I could not find anything I liked, either on the satellite or the local channels. The Gulf War was over now, so I couldn't watch any American or British or French airplanes bombing military targets in Iraq with perfect precision. I couldn't watch Baghdad's sky in total chaos—darkness periodically interrupted by flashes of light, signifying that a military target had been hit. I felt regretful about that. I felt regretful for having missed out on so many exciting nights because I had waited for so long before purchasing a TV. The Lebanese civil war was over too, so what could the local channels possibly show that night? Nothing! They were filling airtime with useless shows that went on for hours. The shows featured young, half-naked women, flaunting their faces, arms, and thighs in order to seduce viewers in the Gulf and keep them glued to their television screens, as one of the local papers here had noted.

I kept switching from one channel to another until I came across a beautiful scene: the profile of a woman I knew. It was Meryl Streep sitting with her head buried in her hands, a wedding ring on her finger. It was like a photo that I had seen once somewhere, perhaps in a book. Her face seemed to hold a secret, an inner peace. It was gorgeous. Her heavy eyelids fluttered slowly. That scene lasted for a few short seconds I enjoyed tremendously. During that time, the woman uttered just one sentence. I assumed she said, "I love you," but there might have been another word that I did not catch at the end of that expression. Perhaps it was the name of the person with whom she had been talking, her son, as I eventually found out.

I don't know any English except for a few words and phrases that are so commonly used they have become part of our Arabic language. Things like "okay" and "darling" and "wow" and "TV." And, of course, there is "I love you," which everybody knows, especially when said slowly and clearly. I confirmed that's what she had said when the camera revealed a child, most likely a little boy, lying in bed in front of her.

I concluded that the scene I was witnessing was that of a woman tucking her child into bed and enjoying a moment of serenity. But what was interesting was that the woman did not seem dressed for bed herself; she didn't look like she had changed out of her day clothes even. Rather, she looked like she was on her way out. The fact that she seemed to be on her way out didn't change my speculation that she was a mother tucking in her child and telling him "I love you" as he dozed off to sleep. After all, going out at night is an old-time habit common to many American women ever since . . . God knows since when! It's very common because women there are just like men. They work during the day and go out at night.

The scene captured my attention because it was beautiful and because it struck me as peaceful and reassuring. And I like Meryl Streep, too. The scene of a woman tucking her son in bed is a magnificent sight, something I might ultimately never experience because my woman—I mean my wife—deserted me, and we hadn't even been married more than a month. True, I had done something that was repulsive and unacceptable and indecent, or whatever you want to call it, but it wasn't a good enough reason for a woman to leave her husband and go back to her parents' house. No reason in the world can make it okay for a woman to leave her husband— unless he puts her in harm's way. If a woman finds herself with a crazy man, then of course she should divorce him.

I was so relieved to see that Meryl Streep had indeed told her son "I love you." How precious motherhood must be: full of tenderness and sacrifice and selflessness. In America, a country of freedom and moral looseness, a woman can still be tender, make sacrifices, and take care of her home. It truly makes me happy that there is still a place for tenderness and motherhood in America because here, the minute people achieve a minimum level of literacy, they start referencing American ideals about women's liberation and equality. As for my wife, she was upset because allegedly I had "tried to rape the neighbors' innocent, sick daughter!" Sometimes, she would go even further with her allegations and claim that I actually did rape her and may have gotten her pregnant, too.

"I refuse for my children to have a biological brother or sister people refer to as a bastard," she had said. "Even if her family made her get an abortion, my children would still have a dead brother or sister."

My wife was against abortion then! I had not known that because we never discussed the topic. She obviously considered an aborted baby a dead child. That was a new piece of information I learned about her.

Then the camera panned over to a man sitting in his office. It was Dustin Hoffman in his workplace, undoubtedly, with feet set up on his desk, talking to his friend sitting across from him. Manners in America are remarkably different from ours when it comes to certain things. That's when I decided I must have been watching

WHO'S AFRAID OF MERYL STREEP?

that divorce movie starring Dustin Hoffman and Meryl Streep. It was my chance to actually watch it. I wondered if I'd be able to follow it all the way to the end when I couldn't understand even one word. Dustin Hoffman was talking quickly and he had a lot to say, so I couldn't understand a thing. I tried to listen carefully in the hope that I would make out a word I did recognize so I could speculate about the rest, but it was in vain. All I could hear was noise, a barrage of noise that sounded somewhat familiar. I could not make out a thing of what he was saying—except for one word: Taxi! Taxi! He said it when he left with his friend (or was that his colleague?), but I did not understand whether he was hailing a cab because he was in a hurry or because he was already late for an appointment, or because he was in the habit of going home by taxi. After all, Americans are rich, and they treat themselves to such luxuries, especially since most cab drivers there are from Third World countries and cab rides are reasonably priced.

How could they possibly broadcast that movie in our part of the world without subtitles? How is that logical? It would not cost more than a hundred dollars to translate a movie like that one. Strange! I didn't know what those TV station owners were even thinking, broadcasting American movies without subtitles. Or did they just assume that whoever watched these kinds of movies must know English? Or, did globalization mean that we had become part of an American territory or that we had suddenly mastered English? Go figure! That channel might as well have been Turkish or Polish or Dutch. Who the hell knew?

When Dustin Hoffman got home, Meryl Streep was waiting for him. She was sitting there, apprehensive and ready, with her bag beside her. She was smoking a cigarette and looking sad and deep in thought. Was she traveling somewhere all of a sudden, after hearing of a relative's death—a father or a mother, a brother or a sister? Then she was startled by a knock at the door and got up to open it. He came in (as was his habit?), kissed her quickly on the mouth (She must be his wife, then! So why did he knock at the door? Doesn't he have a key to his house, and isn't he her husband?), and headed for the phone to make a phone call. She waited for him to finish his call, and her face looked like she was about to tell him something that was hard for her to say. She was looking at him strangely. She said something while he was still talking, so he blocked one of his ears so he could listen to the phone with the other ear. When he was done with his phone call, she started taking things out of her pocket and putting them on the table, after dangling them in front of his eyes first so he could see them clearly: first came the key, then a number of cards that Americans are known for carrying. Then she grabbed her bag and headed for the door. He tried to stop her by taking away her bag, so she left without it. Then he tried to stop her from taking the elevator, but after some going back and forth, she stepped inside the elevator and waited for the elevator door to close.

During that time, they exchanged a lot of words, none of which I got, not even one letter. My God, what was going on? What was happening between these two people on my television screen that I had bought after such a hassle? What was going on between them in my own house? It looked like she was leaving against his will, so who was he? And, who was she? What did they mean to each other? A married couple with an only child? Why was Meryl Streep—this beautiful woman, who, seconds ago, was tucking in her child with a tenderness strong enough to face an army—leaving?? Could a woman like her just leave her son and take off? What did they say to each other? Did she want to go back to her ex-husband, or was she leaving so she could go live with her new lover? Could such a tender mother do such a thing? What was going on then? Did she find out that her husband was having an affair? Did she discover that he had homosexual tendencies?

Please, Meryl Streep, no. Don't take my wife's side! I love you and adore you and tell you right out—even though you might think I'm naïve—that secretly I consider myself the (one and only) suitable man whose shoulder you can cry on.

When the elevator door closed, hiding that beautiful, weeping face from me—that face struck with sadness and concern—the advertisement that came on the television took me by surprise. I realized that the movie had captivated me. I had become absorbed by it despite not understanding a single word! All I knew of the story from the little I had heard before was that the husband and wife get a divorce for some reason and the wife wins the case against her husband in court and that the judge's ruling caused a controversy in America. But I didn't know that Meryl Streep leaves her house that way and leaves her young son behind with his father. I really needed to see the film with subtitles. I just could not follow it without translation. I was not that much of a masochist.

I find Meryl Streep very beautiful and attractive. I enjoy watching her perform. Dustin Hoffman is a very convincing and intelligent actor, too, but as a man he doesn't really go with Meryl Streep. With his long hair, he looked like one of those 1960s intellectuals, the ones who had two long things going for them: their hair and their dicks. In terms of looks, he was nowhere near her. He was more like one of those cheap porn actors who would not draw your attention if you saw them with their clothes on. They are chosen for one reason and one reason only—their huge dicks. It seems to me that a woman like Meryl Streep would only marry a man like Dustin Hoffman out of sympathy or because she did not realize her own true worth. Also, men like him like to play with such women's minds. They fill them with all sorts of delusions and basically buy them. That kind of guy makes even the finest woman believe he's a real big shot, the master of the universe: rich, capable, hope incarnate. The worst part is that the moment he gets the woman, he stops giving her the respect she deserves.

I think the man who had poked his head into the office was reminding Dustin Hoffman about the time. Maybe he had said, "Aren't you going to be late?" Or, "Do you know what time it is?" Because Dustin Hoffman immediately checked his watch and got up before finishing up whatever he had been doing. Did the guy know all about his wife's situation, and that she was feeling neglected? What kind of a husband depended on friends to remind him about his domestic duties? About his duties toward his wife? Had Meryl Streep gone to this guy to complain about her problems? Wouldn't that have caught her husband's attention and lead him to ask her about the meaning of her intimate friendship with his friend or his colleague? Or was it Dustin Hoffman who had been talking to his colleagues at work about his wife's constant complaining, the way lots of men do as part of a kind of conspiracy they have against their wives? That kind of thing is especially true in our part of the world. Take Abu Zaheed, for example, my coffee shop friend. In the middle of our conversation, he would say that whenever he gets upset with his wife, he "rams her with it!" She doesn't like it from behind, so he grabs her by the hair, flips her over, and rams it into her just like that!

What shame!

What shame to talk about such things and divulge the secrets of married life, especially what goes on in the bedroom between a man and his wife. That is absolutely unacceptable.

And this practice of his is especially shameful!

He whinnies with laughter like a horse, going on about his wife. It's an unbearable situation. If I were his wife, I'd divorce him in a second. I'd leave him immediately.

As for that other woman, that angel Meryl Streep, if she were to ask me to choose a man for her—a husband, I mean—it would be very difficult, nearly impossible for me to do. But if I were forced to choose one for her, I would wish her to have someone I care for and admire. I'd wish her to have me. Who better than me? Saying such a thing didn't detract from my love for my wife, though, because it was all just hypothetical and had nothing to do with reality. It was just my way of expressing a desire that could never be realized, because for something like this to really happen would require a thousand and one conditions. It didn't detract from my love for my wife because in all honesty, I was writhing in pain from her having left me. I was burning atop a flaming ember, as if all the love songs had been written for me. Up until the day before, I had mocked those songs "that make you want to vomit!"—as I used to describe them. Now, though, I'd been forced to change my opinion because they struck me right in the heart! But that didn't mean I'd been weakened. On the contrary, in order to come out of my predicament a winner, I had to derive strength from that pain. It was the only way to prevent what had happened the day before from being repeated in the future and becoming a habit of hers, to leave me like that whether she had good reason or not.

The truth was that when my wife left me, I discovered how deep my feelings for her really were. It was a truth I couldn't possibly deny, since I already knew I'd begun to fall for her and had pledged my love to her often, to which she'd responded that my words reminded her of the writings of great poets.

That time when I gave her a gold necklace and clasped it around her neck, as I watched it lay there, dangling down between her breasts so beautifully, I said to her, "The price of gold just went up!"

My love for my wife didn't detract from my total fascination with the film, either.

As I waited for the commercial to end, I was preoccupied with one thought: Where was Meryl Streep going now? It concerned me so much I couldn't think of anything else. I imagined myself being in just the right place to bump into her. In my mind, that place where I happen to bump into the woman of my dreams is always on the road between Tripoli and Beirut. It's cold and rainy outside, and the Queen of Class just happens to be standing out there without a suitcase, trying to protect herself from the gusty winds with her hands. I stop my car for her. She's hesitant at first, but with one brief look into my eyes in which she peers right into my soul and discovers my benevolent nature, she decides to get in the car. Meryl Streep had now become the woman of my dreams, the one I'd been dreaming about for many long years.

I didn't recall how long ago I'd started having that dream. Maybe it was when I started feeling the urgency to get married and that every minute that passed, from that moment forward, was only going to make it harder.

Back in my fantasy, I'm in my car on my way from Tripoli to Beirut. I'm going pretty fast, not because I'm in a hurry, but because the speed keeps my senses perked up. A woman of just the right age—just under thirty—who you can tell is a real lady and is beautiful in the way I like a woman to be beautiful, with a full figure, exactly the kind of woman a man like me dreams of, appears. I pull over without her actually signaling to me. It's the first time I have ever stopped for a woman in my life. Usually I stop to pick up a soldier or a religious cleric or a nun—you know, the kind of person who isn't going to cause problems and at the same time gives you the opportunity to show your good will. I'm not at all troubled when I pull over this time, as if I'm used to stopping whenever I see a

44 woman hitchhiking on the side of the road. She approaches the car, bends down, and after greeting me says, "Beirut?"

"Hop in!" I exclaim.

She gets settled in her seat and immediately says, "You don't seem too troubled even though this is the first time you've ever picked up a woman."

Oh my God! Is she an enchantress or a prophetess?

"If you're really serious, I'm ready to marry you this second. Take me, I'm yours!" She says this with a combination of excitement, bashfulness, and determination. And it's clear she's fully aware of what she's saying. She's fully aware of how bizarre it is, but she's determined to say it anyway! So I keep driving while an unstoppable feeling wells up inside me that happiness is right there and that I'm holding it in my hands. Chance! How lovely chance is. How wonderful for things to just happen on their own without having to venture or be cautious or hesitate, or calculate gains and losses.

I try not to give in to excessive feelings of joy to avoid feeling disappointed and crushed later on, but her words break down all my defenses. I ask her how she knew I was single, and she says, "I had no reason to think otherwise. And besides, in your heart you're single, even if you are married and living with your wife. I'd bet my life on that." ("Actually, I'd bet my every last hope on that, after everything that's happening to me now, and after everything my husband's done to me!" She says that referring to the film.)

Then I say, "What about children?"

"You would be a loving and tender father," she says. "Completely devoted to your children. There's no way in the world you could father children with a woman you didn't feel was yours, was your possession. Yes. Are you listening? She'd have to be yours for all eternity. And if she wasn't and you were to get her pregnant, you would realize immediately that you'd made a mistake and would never let it happen again!"

Her words knock me for a loop. "Am I going to have a boy or a girl?" I ask.

"I'd always wanted a girl," she says. "But now, after taking you into consideration, I'm hoping you have a boy because you deserve peace of mind." She says that last part with utmost conviction and with such kindness it makes my pulse speed up just a little. And my body temperature goes up a noticeable amount! When we reach Dawra on the outskirts of Beirut, I say, "I never asked you where you'd like me to take you because I didn't think you'd have anything against continuing on with me to my house . . . so we can get to know each other better."

"I have to admit I'm not quite sure, but I'm not completely against it, either. I've been very open and frank with you, more than ever before in my life. It's no big secret to tell you it's not a small matter for me to meet some stranger on the street, like him right away, and go home with him. I'm not that kind of a woman, no matter how Western-minded and liberated I might seem. Deep down, I'm 'homegrown,' you hear? I'm a homegrown local when it comes right down to it." She shakes her fist as she says "homegrown," the way people do when they want to prove how sure they are of what they are saying. Then she adds, "I am a child of this good and giving land, and my roots run deep into it."

I imagine that what this woman is saying is dangerous. Very dangerous. Am I in a dream or what? I think about pinching myself like characters do in the *Thousand and One Nights*, like when a common person can't believe what's happening around him is real. Could he really be in the house and arms of a breathtakingly beautiful princess?

I tell her I'm not asking her to make any final decisions yet, just to trust me. To simply trust me. "Just trust me," I say. "Let me be in charge for just an hour." She takes my hand, which I forgot existed until she took it suddenly between hers, like a sacred offering, one that if she ever mistreated it would sabotage her own femininity, her own purity—and everything on which her sense of integrity and pride were founded, her sense of honor and pride in herself, her family, and her land. How could I stop this flood of happiness from breaking through the doors to my inner self? In a few seconds, the contents of my inner self are transformed like a container that has been emptied and refilled with holy water. It was happiness that flooded my soul—I know very well what happiness is. Happiness is when a woman, perfect in every sense of the word, takes your hand and holds it between her silken hands as if it were the gift of ethereal love, with the affection you have always craved.

She agrees to come home with me. But which home?

At this moment in the dream, I always run into the issue of the house. Where would I take her now that she has agreed to come home with me when I actually live with my mother in our family house and don't have a house of my own? I wish our lifestyle were like people's in the West, where you could invite a girl over to your parents' house and just be with her in the privacy of your own room. Instead, I lived with a mother whose only concern, since my father's death, was to blab on me to my aunt every time she happened to find some stuff on my underwear that accidentally spilled out of me during the night. Seeing these things put her out of sorts! My aunt told me it upset my mother so much that sometimes she threw my underwear in the trash. Once my aunt brought this to my attention, I became more careful, and made sure to remove all traces of it. The problem actually started when my mom mistakenly put some metallic object in our expensive Candy washing machine one time, which ruined the rubber lining around its glass door. She ended up paying a lot of money to fix it, so after that she inspected every single thing before putting it inside the washer. She would put the laundry into the machine one item at a time. The problem was that sometimes a person didn't really pay attention and just took off his clothes and carelessly threw them into the laundry basket. Once, she saw one of those stains on the backside of my underwear, so she got worried and started watching me closely to see if there was another stain. And when she found a stain a second and a third time, she started doubting my masculinity. She had no qualms about discussing it with my aunt. The funny part was that she started crying and singing sad songs lamenting her luck. She automatically assumed I was a lost child and issued verdicts about me in absentia. She confided in my aunt that she had suspected me ever since I was a child and that she had been in deep sorrow about it throughout my teenage years because I always used to take on female roles when my friends and I would act out a movie that we had seen on television or in the theater. One time, when she saw my "husband" or "fiancé" or some man kissing me on the mouth and me surrendering to his kiss "like those whores did in the movies," she hit me with unforgettable brutality! My aunt tried to convince her that her concerns were

unfounded and that I was straight and could never be gay. When
my mom asked her how she could be so sure, my aunt felt cornered.
How can a person prove something that cannot be proven? For
months, my mom kept secretly asking about my friends and about
their romantic involvements and female acquaintances.

Once, she said to me, "None of your friends live a normal life!"

"What do you mean normal life?" I said. "They all live
normal lives."

"No," she said. "None of them has a girlfriend."

"How do you know that?" I asked. "And what planet do you
come from? Since when do men talk about their relationships with
women in our culture?"

How could my mother be saying that, my mother who would
get upset if she saw a girl wearing a short dress? She would even
spit in public, warding off the devil from herself and whoever
was accompanying her, whenever she saw a man and a woman in
a "compromising position." For her, a compromising position
meant a man walking down the street with his arm around a woman
or a man and a woman holding hands. "People have no reverence
for God anymore," she would say. During the time she thought I
was gay, however, she got nostalgic for the sight of those young men
and women together. On top of all that, she considered me a sissy
gay man. She assumed that I was not the male *doing* the deed but the
female having it *done to* her. She got so carried away that she recalled
the days I used to play soccer with my classmates, noting how I only
liked to play the goalie position! My aunt laughed so much when
my mother told her that because it took her a while to get it. In my
mother's mind, what connected a goalie and a female was the fact
that they were both targets, about to be penetrated by something,
and waiting for that something to happen while others initiated it.

Oh my God, what a fabulous imagination! What a sick
imagination! Yes, sick. Why couldn't a person's mother have a sick
imagination? Only a sick imagination could take a person that far.
It was unbelievable.

"Oh, come on," my aunt would say. "Have you ever looked
closely at those goalies? They're all manly enough to satisfy an entire
Women's Association." I had no idea where my aunt got such ideas.

Whenever I would reach that point in my dream—the part where I bring the woman home—I would wake up from my beautiful trance, preoccupied with the issue that disturbed me to the core: the house! I had always dreamed of having my own house, where I could come and go as I pleased and where I could have anybody I wanted come visit. And now that my wife had left me, my dream had become a reality. My house was still mine since the lease was in my name. And this dream, which I had been having since I started feeling that I needed to hurry up and get married, is still my most recurring dream every time I give in to exhaustion or boredom or despair. Would this dream ever become a reality? Impossible! Still, I was preoccupied with Meryl Streep and where she would go after leaving her husband and son. During the commercial break, I kept wondering where a woman like her would go—a woman who had left her home because she could no longer deal with her husband's neglect, a woman who was forced to take that last step after everything else had failed, a woman so beautiful and tender and delicate. Anybody who saw her lean over her son and kiss him with such purity would feel his heart break and wouldn't believe that she would ever leave her home—unless she was completely fed up.

That was obvious.

There was a huge difference between the fabric of Meryl Streep's being and that of her husband's. She was way out of his league. When he talked, he sounded crazy. I completely understand why parents feel disappointed when they give birth to a daughter. God knows who girls might fall for! I don't wish for a daughter, not because I don't like girls or because I'm traditional and conservative. I want to spare myself these sorts of problems. Plus, Meryl Streep's husband wasn't anything like those blond actors who exude light and stardom every time they flash their radiant smiles.

Was Meryl Streep going to her parents' house as my wife had done?

Based on the news I was getting, it seemed that my wife was happy at her parents' house.

How could Meryl Streep leave her son with her husband and not take him with her? She should have taken him with her. It would have been better for her. But maybe if she had tried taking

him with her, her husband wouldn't have let her go. Or maybe—
and why should this hypothesis be so far-fetched?—maybe she was
going to her lover who did not want to hear anything about her
husband's son. Who knew what the woman was hiding! In that part
of the world, no one can stop a woman from leaving her husband
and moving in with another man. A woman has the right to do that.
I could only hope she wasn't going to her lover's place. In fact, I
hoped she would ultimately go back to her husband and son—to her
family. It was true that her husband was of a much lower caliber,
and that she was capable of getting a man a thousand times better
than him—even as a divorced single mother—but the mistake had
already been made. Now that she was married to him and had his
child, she couldn't solve the problem by walking out and leaving her
son. Two wrongs don't make a right. I said this while deep down I
didn't want her to go back to him because he was not the right man
for her at all. But there was no other choice.

There was no other choice for her but to go back to her husband.
But before that, she would have to teach him a lesson so he could
really know who she was and learn not to overstep his boundaries.
He must know that she would stay with him not because he was such
a catch, but because she had self-respect and would never go back
on her word, and because the most important thing for her was the
happiness of her son, the light of her life.

Oh, my God. If I had a woman like her, I would never slight
her in any way.

I kept thinking that was what she should do in the end. Until
then, however, she had to be patient and keep him guessing until
she figured out how good his intentions really were. She had to
leave him anxious until he admitted his mistake and repented.
That's what I thought my wife was doing, even though she's no
Meryl Streep, and I—luckily—am no Dustin Hoffman.

I had been expecting her to come around to my point of view
after just a couple of days. I thought she would accept my explanation
of the events—my apology, rather—and come back home. Back
to her home. And be pleased with herself, as others would be
pleased with her. Indeed, all the angels in heaven would be pleased
with her.

I expected her to come back and embark on a renewed relationship with me.

But a week? A month? Two months!

If she was trying to teach me a lesson, the lesson was learned. She had spent more time away from home at her mother's than a husband could bear. It was long enough for me to learn the lesson and long enough for her to get over it. And besides, I promised her that from now on she could have everything her way. That was assuming something actually had gone on—that I had actually tried something with that girl. But I had denied that and told her nothing had happened. So what plausible argument did she have against going back on her decision to not come home, a decision she had made as a new bride in a frenzied state of anger?

When I realized the movie I was watching was none other than *Kramer vs. Kramer*, I changed the channel in a sort of mechanical, involuntary way, as if to prevent my wife from seeing it because she loved those kinds of movies and stories and that kind of talk.

"As soon as we get a TV, we're getting cable," she'd say. "So we can get dozens of stations, even more than my parents." She said that because the cable companies blocked a number of explicit channels from a certain type of clientele—like her parents, for example. She wasn't about to be deprived of anything, especially not the stations that showed the risqué programs and movies. If it hadn't been for some sense of shame in front of me, she'd have bought the TV before the fridge! Maybe before the bedroom set. No, *definitely* before the bedroom set, because there were quite a few times when she would have slept on the couch out in the living room if I hadn't insisted she come to bed—if I hadn't threatened her and warned her of the consequences of such behavior.

"Oh yeah?" she asked me once. "And what are the consequences of such behavior?"

"A broken home," I answered.

"You mean ours is intact?"

Once she wouldn't budge; she spent the whole night out on the couch. In the morning, she got up, put her clothes on in a hurry, and headed to her mother's to finish sleeping over there. She used to do that over the tiniest thing. The flimsiest excuse.

Whether she had a reason or not. She was only punishing herself, sleeping all alone on the couch, forsaking her own bed and all the tenderness and attention I showed her there. Like a queen. I treated her like a queen! Including the first time I went all the way with her— "opened her up," as they say. That was after we had moved to our new apartment and after I waited patiently over many days and nights. It had been a huge shock to me, totally unexpected, that first night. I was talking to her as a groom to his new bride since it was our first real night together as a man and a woman in every sense of the word. We were sharing what we knew about wedding nights and about virginity and its significance and how some cultures don't give it much importance, unlike ours, which prefers the girl to be a virgin, unsullied, because a virgin is pure of memory in a way, and there's nothing that might cause her love to be divided between her husband and some other man. A girl who occasionally strays from our customs out of recklessness or some other reason and loses her virginity might resort to having the torn hymen sewn back up so she can get married. Otherwise, no one will have her. My wife had refuted that, saying that a lot of girls nowadays refuse to do that and wouldn't marry a man who didn't accept them the way they were.

"A lot of girls?" I questioned.

"Relatively!"

I retorted that it was a rare occurrence and only happened in certain circles and was therefore negligible.

This had been our conversation as we lay in bed, mere moments before I penetrated her, before I opened her up and tore her hymen and deflowered her. "Be careful!" she said to me, when I was completely engrossed, not knowing where to begin and where to end. "Don't treat me like some stolen car you'll never be able to register legally. Take me slowly. Treat me like a car you have to pay for in installments." I loved the way she pointed out to me what she liked. I did what she said out of respect for her feelings and a desire to share with her that rare pleasure that would happen only once in a lifetime, to me and to her. But despite all my good intentions, every time I tried to go inside her she would wince, forcing me to withdraw and try all over again.

She truly didn't want me to ravish her. She wanted to put off complete intercourse, maybe wait a week or two or more, during which time we could be satisfied with foreplay. It would also give us time to prepare ourselves mentally. And sometimes she would say prepare ourselves physically. When I showed my bewilderment at the word "physically," she would respond that it was all connected. But how long of a delay were we talking about? For days she'd been asking me to be patient, and for days I had obeyed and accepted waiting. But for how long? Come on!

I hadn't yet fully grasped that putting things off was part of her nature. She had wanted to postpone the wedding, so we delayed it. Then she wanted to wait a few more weeks, but I flat out refused because the preparations had been made, so what was the point? We had rented and furnished the apartment. What else could we need? I was thirty-five, and she was thirty. Why would we wait? For years I had not been able to make up my mind. I had not been able to narrow it down to a particular girl. I had given up looking for the perfect match. But now it had finally happened. Now that I had decided to get married and started dreaming of a baby that in nine months' time would become the light of my life, I was not going to back down. And besides, her fertile years were nearing their end, so why did she want to wait any longer?

"What's the hurry?" was the answer she gave me. That was her one and only answer. I used to get annoyed by that excuse, or rather that non-excuse. That strange position of hers really made me mad because it wasn't convincing to anybody, not even her mother who was always on her side, except on that topic. Her mother never disagreed with her on anything except that! But I wish she had! I wish she had encouraged her to postpone the wedding. Maybe the whole thing would have fallen apart. Maybe we wouldn't have gotten to where we were now.

"Put your trust in God, my daughter. These are matters that can't be postponed." That's what her mother used to say to her with a sharp tone despite the fact that she was an extremely open-minded woman who accepted new ideas with excitement and sometimes even with passion. Even at seventy she still loved life, loved to socialize, and loved to smoke. She smoked a lot and drank beer! She loved the singer Sabah. She really loved her, but in a very special way. For example, if she heard Sabah was going to be on television in the evening, she would get herself ready to stay up late to watch her. She would laugh with all her heart. She would be in tears with laughter. She would call her by her pet name, Sabbouha, and she would dance. She'd get all worked up sitting on the couch when Sabah sang that one song that had the word Sabbouha in it, and she'd start slapping her thighs and lifting and lowering her skirt, as if it was the middle of summer and she was all alone in the room trying to cool herself off.

And so we got married and moved into our house at my insistence and under her mother's pressure. My aunt, however, kept silent about the issue, never voicing any opinion, even though during that period my wife never missed a daily visit with my aunt. So strange!

She finally agreed to the wedding date without pressure from anybody. I was as candid with her as I could be and told her that if she didn't want to get married to just say so, in the presence of her parents, my mother, my aunt, and all our relatives. She stated clearly and unequivocally that she wanted to get married. But there were times when we went out together alone that she would ask me not to push the issue. It was odd how she suddenly felt so strong when it was just the two of us. When she got me alone, she always had the upper hand, which was why I always tried to make sure that any binding statements she made would be made in front of all the relatives, particularly her mother, so it would be difficult for her to go back on her word. Sometimes I would corner her and force her to voice an opinion she secretly held, such as it being too soon to have a baby, for example. She wanted to put off getting pregnant "until the right time," and so I made sure to bring up such subjects out in the open so that if she revealed her opinion, everyone would rebuff her.

"When will the right time be?" they'd all chime in.

Getting back to her being ready "mentally" and "physically," I showed a lot of patience, waiting many long days while she got herself ready. I even sought the advice of trustworthy religious men, among other people. They all advised me to take it easy but to also be firm.

They advised me to use my tongue for words and other things, and to use my hands, and to be gentle and kind and firm and never waver.

Finally I told her I wasn't going to wait a second longer. We had talked for a long time in bed—about issues of virginity and so on—and I caressed her all the while, as you would a young bride, having taken into consideration all the advice I had gotten on the topic. My desire grew intolerable, and after a few attempts after which I was forced to retreat because of all her moaning and screaming, I rammed inside her like a bullet, not caring that her teeth had sunk into my shoulder. Blood flowed from both of us, but she bled more profusely. She cried and recoiled from me, hiding under the covers, while I wiped the blood off of myself with a few tissues from the Kleenex box by the bed. I went to the bathroom and came back with a towel, which I used to wipe the blood off of her, but she took it from me and covered up the body parts that I had exposed. When she asked me later why I had wiped off the blood with a towel and not with Kleenex, I did not tell her the real reason. I just said it was cleaner that way.

Later, as I was taking a shower, I inspected the blood residue on me since I couldn't do that in our bedroom, where it was too dark to see well because the sun was going down and the shutters were closed, of course. I also checked out the towel, which I had absentmindedly returned to its place, instead of putting it in the laundry basket. When I came back into the room, she was still crying, so I tried to console her and make her feel better. When she had calmed down, and without either of us planning to, we went back to talking about virginity and other related issues. At some point in the conversation, I told her what happened to a girl who had been dating a friend of mine. My friend confided in me that he had deflowered the girl and then refused to marry her because she had let him do it. The woman who was going to be his wife and the mother of his children had to be perfect before marriage. "Her blood should be mixed with his blood alone," he had said. This girl really loved him and was ready to give him everything she had, her only condition being that he would love her back and be pleased with her. He told me he took her virginity in stages—unlike what he had done later with his wife on their wedding night.

He had ambushed his wife like a wild beast and brutally deflowered her, fiercely tearing up her hymen. Despite the fact that she was bleeding, or, maybe because she was bleeding, she begged him to stay inside her and not pull out. "That's how it should be with your wife the first time," he said. "You should tear her up and break her and violate her, but with chivalry and integrity, not like a barbarian." So, yes, with his girlfriend he had been patient and had taken his time. He completed his mission after several attempts, pushing deeper each time, so she would not feel too much pain and so he could deny what happened in case she blamed him for it. But she never blamed him, and he did not have to deny anything. She simply left him after she lost all hope, having surrendered to him and given him the most precious thing she possessed.

The problem occurred when another young man asked for her hand in marriage. She had known him as a friend for a long time, and he wanted to marry her right away, so she said yes. She had not realized he was in such a rush, so she hurried to the doctor without telling anyone, including her closest friends. The doctor took advantage of her when he found out how desperate she was to sew up her hymen. She got married a few days after her surgery even though the doctor warned her not to have full intercourse for at least two weeks, preferably three. But sometimes the winds blow in the opposite direction desired by ships! The man could not understand why his wife wanted to wait, and she was completely unable to put it off, so she just let him have his way even though she was at risk of having a hemorrhage or an infection. She actually did hemorrhage and had to be taken to the hospital. Luckily, she was able to contact the same doctor who had done the surgery. She had anticipated this and was generous with him and gave him all he asked for, so he took care of her and treated her case with extreme decency and utmost discretion.

That was not the point of the story, however. The point of the story was that after this man had deflowered his bride he noticed a tiny thread stuck to his penis, which made him wonder, so he asked her about it. At that moment, he was so anxious he seemed like he was about to burst into flames. She answered him nonchalantly that it must have come off his or her clothes. "What else could it be?"

she remarked. He inspected the thread as he lifted it to his eyes and dangled it in front of the two of them; then he tossed it. As for her, she almost fainted from fear! Her heart almost stopped, and for a moment she forgot all about her pain.

Her husband was so thrilled by the sight of blood on himself and her that he hugged her tightly, thanking God for having him in his good graces, and she loved it. As he wiped the blood off himself and her, he happily gazed at it. For the first time, she understood how much it means to a man that a woman save herself for him. It is a precious gift!

"Why are you telling me this now?" my wife asked. Her question took me by surprise, and I got anxious. I knew that she felt my anxiety, but I did not say anything. I hesitated before asking her the question that would trigger her anger.

"Was it too painful?"

I couldn't understand why that question roused her anger. After all, what else would newlyweds possibly talk about? How could my asking about the most important thing that could happen to a woman in her lifetime—the loss of her virginity—be considered irrelevant? What question could be more crucial than this one? It was my duty to ask her about this in order to alleviate her pain, the pain that I myself had caused her! This question was not just crucial—it was the main issue.

But she was able to contain her anger, or so it seemed to me at the time. She stopped herself from saying anything that she would regret, despite her persistent pain and bleeding. That was a sign that she was a woman whose highest priority was to hold on to her marriage.

She turned her face away from me. That was all she did.

But why did she do that? It was strange.

I thought we'd talk about this subject for a long time—and with indescribable delight. Or had she sensed my worry and gotten mad? What gave her the feeling that I was worried? I had clearly shed her blood, which was all I wanted. She had clearly been in pain as I did that. Come to think of it, she had been in an awful lot of pain.

When my friends and I were at the peak of our youth, we weren't preoccupied with the issue of virginity. We were just turned on by it. Quite frankly, even today, I still do not know a woman who has had premarital sex. I know a few stories from the newspaper and movies about women who had premarital sex, and those stories always end with an honor crime, especially in the movies. We never discussed this issue when we were young because remaining a virgin until marriage was the assumption. There was no need to point it out, the way one did not point out something as natural as breathing.

Only once was this topic broached openly. We were riding in an electric car at the time. No doubt it was the only car of its kind in Beirut, and our friend had stolen the key from the pocket of his environmentally-conscious father. We were stopped at a red light when a girl with very skimpy clothes crossed in front of us. We all felt embarrassed. Our friend driving the car said, "I'd rape that girl if I caught her in the right place." We responded that no one would marry her after that. Then I interjected, with some exaggeration and humor, that virginity was now a thing of the past. But he said, "There's no way I would marry someone who's not a virgin. I get to deflower at least one. It's my right!"

"Mine too," I thought to myself. It was something I could have easily said out loud.

On that historic night, my wife had spent the night on the living room sofa with towels and cotton bandages between her thighs. Several Kleenex tissues and the free raffle ticket that came with the box lay discarded on the floor even though she was the one who always insisted that I never toss any of the tickets because she was hoping to win a 2000 Polo Volkswagen. She also had some medications and lotions by her side. Undoubtedly, she had been anticipating what happened since girls always plan for that very night. She must have asked her mother on the phone what she should do, and I think her mother consulted a friend of hers, a nurse or a pharmacist perhaps. And as a gesture from me to share a pain that I inevitably caused her—a pain that I was almost legally bound to exert—I spent the night on the sofa across from her, despite her insistence that I sleep in the bed and despite her assertion that she would feel more comfortable if I left her alone to take care of the situation. But I insisted on staying with her.

That day, I truly wished we had a television, and I thought to myself that perhaps she was right—having a TV was just as important as having other necessities. I also thought to myself that there was a problem in my relationship with my wife, a problem that I had to acknowledge. There were times when it seemed to me that my wife was right, even when I was initially convinced that she was not. Later, things would happen that would confirm her having been right all along. Take that night for instance. If only we had had a television, we would not have been in that predicament—suffocating!—and our night would have been more pleasant. We would have had some fun at least, despite everything else.

That was a problem that I could not deny.

She went to her mother's the next morning and stayed there the entire day. She would not come back until I went after her myself. Reluctant at first to listen to me, her mother eventually mediated and told her daughter she should go back home with me. At the time, I felt her mother's initial hesitation was a tactic of sorts—to show her daughter she understood her position, just like when she made it sound like it had been all my fault when she said, "You men are always in such a hurry to get what you want. You're all just naturally selfish."

"There are some things," I responded, "that we are obliged to do." To which she replied, "Don't try to teach me about things I know a lot more about than you do! What a pity!"

"What are you so heartbroken about?" I asked her. "Tell me, please. I'd really like to know what big sin I've committed." She responded with the same thing her daughter had said to me the night before, "Don't treat your wife like a stolen car you'll never be able to legally register. Treat her like a car you're paying for in installments!" Apparently my wife didn't come up with those peculiar analogies on her own as I had originally thought. She inherited them from her mother.

A lot of time passed, but despite all my attempts to persuade her, she did not come back home. And she would not talk to me the whole time, either. She would tell her mother to get rid of me somehow, to say, "She's not here," or "She's asleep," or something like that, and she would not come to the phone until I insisted to the point of embarrassment.

This time, though, she was the one who called me!

Rrrrinng, rrrrinng, rrrrinng rang the phone, in a very
ordinary way, and I picked it up, also in a very ordinary way, not
even thinking about who might be calling.

"Hello!"

It was her!

"Listen," she said to me. "Go and work things out with those
neighbors of yours whose daughter you tried to rape and who won't
stop calling me every day, threatening me with all sorts of atrocious
punishments if you don't go to the police and turn yourself in
and own up to what you did to their sister. Listen! My father is
an old man and my brothers are all living abroad. My uncle was
the only one I could turn to who could go to them directly and
tell them there was no longer any relationship binding me to
you and that they should take their complaints to you and you
alone. Understand?"

"Yes, I understand," I said. "I'll take care of my problem with
them on my own. But what do you mean 'no relationship binding
you to me'?"

"I'm filing for divorce. I've already gotten a lawyer who'll serve
you official notice sometime soon."

All this had happened while I went about my business totally
oblivious, waiting like an idiot for her to come back to me, a humble
and subdued woman.

"Let me make it clear as of right now," she said, "I am not
coming back to you, and even without the rape incident I would've
made the same decision. Get it? You go your way, I go mine."

"But what about the baby?" I asked, after which she went silent.
She did not say anything!

A few seconds later she said, "Do you get it?"

"Yes, I get it," I told her, "but answer me about the baby!"
She remained silent again. Finally, after a long pause, she said,
"What baby?"

Oh my God! She said *what baby*!

Before the business about divorce came up, I had been confident
that sooner or later she was going to come back to me because she
was pregnant. I had been sure that she would not spend her entire
pregnancy at her parents' house and have the baby there. That just

would not make sense. But it seemed that she had been lying to everyone about the whole thing, covering it up. How long could she keep that up, though? Her belly was not going to stay nice and flat the way she liked it forever. It was going to grow big and round and, eventually, she would not be able to deny it anymore.

She would have to come back sooner or later. I had been sure of that and would never tire of waiting.

And the baby was going to be a boy, no doubt about it. I had read in a serious scientific journal that sperm consists of two types of cells—male and female—and the female sperm cells live longer than the male cells, but the male sperm cells swim faster and reach the ovum first. That was why I would always pull her pelvis toward me as much as possible when I came in her, and plunge as deeply into her as I could, to shorten the distance between the tip of my penis and the ovum—so the male sperm cells would get there before they perished and gave the longer lasting female ones a chance to surpass them. It was a very successful approach. The baby would be a boy, God willing. When she would ask me why I was lifting her "bottom" up that way, "Like you're trying to pour something into me!" (her *bottom*—how romantic!), I would just keep quiet. I was not about to give away my secret, and I do not regret that at all, especially since she always claimed it did not make any difference to her if it was a boy or a girl, though sometimes I suspected she would rather have a girl. "Why not a girl?" she would say. "Don't you like me? Did you forget I'm a girl? Aren't I 'as beautiful as a spring flower,' doesn't my chest 'make the price of gold go up'?"

"Come here," she said once, dragging me to the mirror, "You want to see for yourself how happy you are with me? Come watch how you ravish me like an animal." Another time, she dragged me to the mirror and said, "Look at yourself. See? You look like an ape!" I could not figure out if she meant that my being a man who preferred sons made me look like an ape, or whether it was my being a very hairy man—one covered from head to toe with thick tufts—that made me like an ape. I knew her majesty preferred those blond Hollywood movie stars on whose sleek bodies you could not find a speck of dust, let alone any hair! But on the other hand, she also thought we Mediterranean types were old-fashioned. She

really had a way of confusing me, that woman. She confused the *61*
hell out of me, set my head spinning, because deep down I really
like for a woman to be shy and sweet and bashful, but in spite of
everything she aroused me. I could spend twenty-four hours a day
in bed with her because the only time I really felt she was mine was
when I was inside her. But even then I felt she was slipping through
my hands and I could not grab hold of her, like quicksilver or a
slippery eel that requires lots of patience and cunning to catch in
your hands.

"Oops, I forgot to call my mother today." That was the kind of
thing she would say out of nowhere, with me inside her, deep inside
her, oblivious in my utter bliss to ever having been born and existed
on this earth. "Aren't you having fun?" I would say, having been
snapped out of my happy state.

"Yes, I am," she would say and add—believe it or not—after
saying yes: "Why do you ask?"

And I would answer her. Once I answered that if she were
indeed having a good time, her mind would not wander off like that
and suddenly remember she forgot to call her mother.

"Well, I'm like a diesel engine. It takes me a while to warm up!"
she said.

In our part of the world, there are two types of engines: diesel
and gasoline. Diesel engines require extra time to warm up before
working at full capacity. Gasoline engines, on the other hand,
heat up right away, but they do not have the endurance of diesel
engines. In other words, she was saying I heat up quickly and I cool
off quickly, too. I get all excited and climax too quickly. That was
the idea she was trying to get across to me. I did not please her, in
other words. She was suffering and had the right to look elsewhere.
She had only one life to live; she had a right to take pleasure in her
life. Why should she deny herself that? For whose sake? Mine? I was
not the kind of man she would sacrifice for, especially not with her
pleasure, with her life.

I wondered who was more American: Meryl Streep or my wife.
Western women may have had a reputation for being brutal, but
my wife was brutal in real life. They act that way in movies and our
women make it a reality!

When my wife found out she was pregnant, she did not tell me, the way a woman usually tells her husband when she finds out she is carrying his child, the way my friend's foreign wife told her husband. "I am so happy that *you* made me pregnant!" She had said to him, "So happy I'm carrying *your* baby inside me." But not my wife—daughter of my own country and member of my own religious group—she did not say anything like that at all. What she said when she realized that she had missed her period was that I was evil! Evil!

"Why am I evil?"

"I didn't get my period!"

My face lit up, and I went to give her a big, reassuring hug, but before I could, she burst into tears and ran to the phone to tell her mother. "Mom. I missed my period!" Her mother said something on the other end, then, "No, no, no! Not like that."

"Why didn't you use a condom?" she said, turning to me. "I can't take birth control pills for medical reasons."

Oh my God! Who had asked her to take birth control pills in the first place? And how did she know she could not take them for medical reasons?

She spoiled it for me, the beauty of being a new father. But despite that, I experienced a moment of happiness that I had never felt in my entire life. I had never felt so happy. There is nothing more beautiful than hearing your wife tell you she is having your baby. And logic dictates that your wife should be as happy as you are, happier even, about the fact that you have gotten her pregnant, that you have made her fertile and transformed her into a mother—the most beautiful thing in the world, the symbol of love, tenderness, giving, and sacrifice. What could be more beautiful and nobler than this? I tried over and over again to find out why she had burst out in tears like someone devastated by a catastrophe. She could not really respond and simply said it was a mysterious feeling, one much more powerful than her, that had caused her such a desire to weep. Honestly, at the time, I kind of liked how she reacted. I concluded that her behavior must have been a result of her innocence and purity, the innocence of a young woman who knew very little about the ways of life. I saw her as one of many other young women who knew very little about the reality of life but who still deserved respect.

Yes, I loved being her gateway to reality—her guide, taking her by the hand and walking her through the hard, muddy, and dangerous pathways so she, the mother of my children, could remain pure.

That was why I was surprised when she asked me about condoms.

The first time she asked me if I liked using condoms, I asked her what a condom was. She said it was male contraceptive. I was surprised. No, I was actually shocked! Did she really not want to have children? What surprised me most was the fact that she used the term "male contraceptive" so naturally and without inhibition. That term had been introduced into our every-day vocabulary by some media outlets, with AIDS being the alleged reason for introducing it in the first place.

That was just a pretext!

Then came the billboards in our public places, featuring different types of condoms in ways that were absolutely shocking to our traditional sensibilities and values. Ours is a conservative society, one that still values things like honor. In fact, there are daily news stories about honor crimes, stories about some woman getting killed by her youngest brother—if her eldest brother fails to do it—or even by her father or son. Just yesterday, we read a story about a man who killed his sister for disobeying him and eloping with the man she loved. Her brother had wanted to marry her off to another man. Yet, they still flaunted these billboards on the sides of our main roads about methods for AIDS prevention, with condoms heading the list. It was as if they were trying to liberate sex from the strict confines of wedlock.

I am not a fundamentalist, but I am a big believer in modesty and discretion. They were treating public spaces completely differently from our private homes. Those ads encouraged people to use male contraceptives (what a name!) when suspecting their partners of infidelity. Personally, I do not see the difference between the bedroom and the television screen. Nor do I see the difference between the television screen and the living room where all the family gathers, in the company of well-intentioned and ill-intentioned guests. What kind of ideas would run through the ill-intentioned guest's mind whenever a commercial promoting the use of condoms appeared on the screen, while your own wife, young daughter, or older sister—whom you know has been dreaming of a

man to brighten up her life—or even your mother, is sitting next
to you? Yes, your own mother. After all, women in our country
used to get married early, often before they even turned twenty, and
often became grandmothers while still very young. In last month's
paper we read that a grandson had killed his grandma because she
was involved in a sexual relationship with a man barely older than
him. Now try to imagine all these women around you in the living
room! Personally, I get shy when these things pop up on the screen
in the presence of a sister, a mother, or any female relative. I do
not even know where to hide, to the point that I try to make myself
shrink. And here was my wife asking me about male contraceptives
just like that, as if she were asking about a bottle of water! Good
thing she said it in English the first time. Saying it in English meant
she did not see it as just another thing or just another term.

It did not matter to me that my wife knew that term. What
mattered was that she had given me the impression she was familiar
with that method of protection and had used it so frequently it had
become something customary or normal.

When I asked her why she was asking about male contraceptives
and what she was scared of, she said, "I'm not scared of anything. I
just don't want us to get ahead of ourselves."

I could not help but ask her if she had used it before, to which
she cleverly replied: "It's for men, not women."

"How do you know that?" I asked.

She just shrugged her shoulders to let me know that she was now
sulking because she was sick and tired of my questions. I was a bore.
When I asked her to answer my question, she started crying.

Yes!

Apparently, my wife had the right to burst into tears should
her husband ask whether or not she had ever used a condom. Her
insides must be somebody else's business, not mine! Incidentally,
how did she know in the first place that birth control pills were not
good for her health?

"From the doctor! The doctor!" she cried. "Haven't you heard
of doctors?"

I had been feeling for quite a while that things were not going
the way I wanted or hoped they would go and that perhaps I had made

the wrong choice. For a long time now, I had been feeling that this woman was not mine and that she had been hiding things that I simply could not accept. With every day that passed, I was drowning further, a little bit at a time. I was helpless. I experienced these foreboding feelings the first time we got together at the Rawda Café, the day after my aunt had introduced us at her house. Back then, I was completely incapable of predicting where this whole thing was heading.

I had called her on her cell phone and told her I had been thinking about her since the day before because, in all honesty, she had caught my eye. I told her the truth. I suggested we meet soon and assured her that I was not one of those conniving people. I believed in honesty as a principle, especially when it came to girls who, like her, were decent people (born and raised in a good family).

We met at the Rawda Café. She came alone in her '83 Honda Accord, and I came in my '92 Volkswagen Jetta. I had deliberately chosen that particular café in order to prove my good intentions. It was a spacious outdoor café with many tables and no secluded spots where couples could hide out of sight. Still, the fact that it was spacious and had plenty of tables provided its customers with a feeling of privacy and intimacy. I really did not want to take her to one of those shady cafés that were scattered all over Beirut, because I wanted to clarify from our very first date that I was not in it just for fun. I wanted to set the record straight that I was serious and that marriage was my goal. I had no doubt that my stance would make her respect me more, because once a woman hits thirty (my aunt had told me her age), marriage becomes her first and foremost goal in life.

The service at that café had been quick, which was not really a problem in itself, but was what sparked the problem between us, because as soon as we sat down, and before we had even had the chance to exchange a few words about whether or not she liked the place, or what she would like to drink, the waiter showed up.

"I'd like a beer," she said before he asked us what we would like, even before he had gotten to our table.

She took me by surprise!

I was truly confused and had no idea what I should do or where to look or what to say. She seemed so assertive and confident, like young men in Lucky Strike commercials or like powerful young women who always get what they want—be it a bottle of perfume or a stiff drink—often defeating men who may be more attractive than they are, because they are just so determined to have their way. She did not even look at me after she had ordered but rather casually started fishing for something in her purse. She pulled out her French cigarettes, Gaulouise Blondes with no filters. Those cigarettes used to be popular among leftists in the late sixties and early seventies, and I rarely saw anyone smoking them these days.

Good thing she did not look at me until after she had ordered because I would not have been able to hide my surprise.

"Pepsi, please," I told the waiter.

I said it as casually as possible so she would not think I was trying to rub it in her face. Despite my surprise, which was not without disappointment, or even dismay, I was able to gauge the situation. We were still at the beginning of the road, and—God willing—everything could still be fixed, especially since she came from a good background and probably knew that men were the guardians of women and that this was just the way God had designed the world and intended it to be.

I had planned on ordering a beer, but I intentionally changed my mind so she would have to drink her beer alone while I drank Pepsi! That way I hoped she might recognize her mistake on her own. But she did not recognize a thing, not even when I ordered the Pepsi, or at least that is how she acted. It was all very normal to her, a man and a woman sitting at a table together, the man drinking a Pepsi and the woman drinking a beer, there at the Rawda Café in southwest Beirut. I am all for helping women get out of the confining snail shell tradition has trapped them in, but at the same time, I still want women to maintain a certain level of decorum. If she had just asked me at least, I would have happily given her permission. I would have encouraged her, even. But for her to go and do whatever she felt like as if I was some kind of scarecrow was something I just could not accept.

At any rate, that little incident passed and we began talking. It was a very nice and refreshing beginning. A person gets caught up in the atmosphere, after all, and does not realize that it is the little things that actually matter. Too bad!

The waiter who brought our drinks was not the same one to take our order. He placed the bottle of beer in front of me and the Pepsi in front of her and left. She looked at the beer in front of me and smiled a little, as though thanking me in advance for what she assumed I would do, which was to fix the waiter's mistake. But I intentionally took my time, giving her a chance to reach the conclusion on her own that the waiter had not really made a mistake but had simply acted very normally and appropriately. She was the one who had made a mistake. After all, we were living over here in our part of the world, not over there in the world of all those movies people watch via satellite. The little smile she had on her face shrank, and she suddenly seemed confused and irritated. Then she stood up suddenly and "excused" herself for a moment. She did not say she was going to the bathroom but rather, "Excuse me for a moment!" And during that moment I felt very bewildered, realizing just how smart she was. Intelligence in a girl like that, I thought, was a characteristic that should not be taken lightly. She should be handled with extra caution and care. Very casually, she had put the ball in my court. So was I supposed to correct the waiter's mistake during her "moment" of absence, or what? While I was thinking about what I should do, I saw a friend of mine over at another table. My savior! I went over and said hello to him and dragged out the conversation way beyond what the situation called for, checking out of the corner of my eye if she had come back to our table, until at last she did come back. I quickly ended my conversation with my friend and went back to our table only to find a second bottle of beer! The Pepsi bottle had been pushed into the middle of the table. I sat down and pushed aside the bottle of beer that had been placed in front of me, grabbed the Pepsi, and started drinking it.

I should have done what Meryl Streep did in the first scene of the film. I should have done it so many months ago after that first meeting in the café. But I had always gone around like someone who had been hit over the head, not knowing where he was and unable to tell right from wrong. What I now saw with absolute clarity had been no more than a foggy, unreliable glimpse of the truth at the time. It had been as if my eyes had been covered with a film.

For example, I did not think for a second that when she had called me "evil" for getting her pregnant that she actually meant what she said. I never thought she really meant I was evil. I thought—well, I wanted to think anyway—that she meant that as a man, I possessed great power and potency. I thought she was alluding to the influence and strength of males in general. I did not comprehend that she truly meant I had hurt her and had changed and transformed her body and that she would never be able to rid herself of the horrible scars I had left on her even after the delivery—they would be there forever. She treated me as if I had splashed her with acid and scarred her for life, or as though I had injected her with something that would kill her. How strange!

The first question I ever asked her, at the start of the conversation during that first famous get-together at the Rawda Café, was: "Are you seeing anyone?" When she looked at me shyly without responding, I said, "In all honesty, I will be very straightforward and open with you, and I'd like you to be the same with me: open and honest from the start." I told her I had never been so frank before in my life and that I'd had many girlfriends and romantic experiences, but they had all been casual and fleeting, for the sake of having some fun and nothing more. I promised to tell her all about them and about everything else in my life, and to not hide anything from my past.

"You don't have to do that," she said. "Your past is yours. It belongs to you."

"Yes, I do," I said. "What belongs to one of us should belong to both of us."

My wife hesitated before giving me an answer after I repeated the question several times. Finally, though, she said, "It's inevitable for a girl to be exposed to certain things at some point in her life."

"Exposed to what?" I asked, probably looking concerned, which was a mistake and might have stopped her from speaking openly. She looked at me with fear and caution.

I said, "Don't worry. Our relationship should be based on honesty."

"It's way too soon for that kind of talk!"

"Everything hinges on your answer to this question."

She looked straight at me and said, "Lots of guys and men of various ages have asked to marry me, and sometimes I would spend time alone with them and meet them just like this."

"That's it?"

She was silent.

I repeated the question, "Is that it?"

She nodded her head, to which I exclaimed, "Well then let's begin!"

She smiled when she saw my cheeks turn red, and she sighed. Then she covered her face with her hands for quite a while before uncovering it. She had tears in her eyes.

"Are those tears of joy or sadness?" I asked.

"Why do you want to know?" she asked angrily.

"Beginnings are always exciting and troubling!" Her heart was so full of joy her eyes overflowed with tears. Her delight poured forth as tears in her eyes.

The second time I called, to ask her out again, she was resistant, which is normal for a single woman in our culture, no matter how liberated she might appear to be. She turned me down, giving me a hundred reasons and excuses why she could not. Eventually my aunt let me in on a secret and showed me the key: You asked too many embarrassing questions the first time at the Rawda Café! You offended her honor and more!

That was a good thing my aunt did. It was a warning to me. I had to be careful how I behaved and what kinds of questions I asked in the future. In a way, I had learned to respect the boundaries.

But it is not as if I forced myself on her, so why did she get married if she did not want to share everything with her husband? Past, present, and future, for better or for worse? Why did she get married if she did not want to have children? And why did she get married if she did not want to have sex with her husband? Why did she get married if she could not put up with her husband making one little mistake (and then turn around and call this trivial incident attempted rape)? Why did she get married if she did not want to be a wife?

Did she get married just so she could get divorced and free herself from the chains put on her as a single woman?

For God's sake!

Or did she get married to cover up the scandal the French guy had introduced into her life (and my aunt's life)?

Could I have been the victim of her carefully studied strategy? What about my aunt? What was her role in all of it?

There was no doubt it had all been a conspiracy in which my aunt played a vital role. A whole week had passed since the crisis exploded and my aunt had not called to ask me what happened or even to check to see if I was all right.

What the heck?

"She's gorgeous!"

"Gorgeous," my aunt said the first time she told me about her neighbors' daughter who lived with her parents in the next building. I was overjoyed by that surprising bit of information. I was overjoyed because I trusted my aunt's taste, too. She was known for her earnestness and for not plunging into quixotic, losing battles, especially when it came to such sensitive topics. My aunt was a woman who resisted her emotions and always acted sensibly.

My aunt had told me that the neighbor's daughter liked her very much, felt comfortable with her, confided in her more than anyone else, and visited her all the time. That, for sure, was what made me hope that everything would work out. But at the same time, this joyful feeling also held me back from asking a number of questions that immediately came to mind, such as why had my aunt waited until then to approach me with the wonderful news. Why hadn't she introduced me to her sooner? Why hadn't she ever mentioned her name before? My aunt lived in that building for two whole years, ever since her husband bought the apartment, not long before he was killed in the oil well fires that had been set at the refinery in Kuwait where he worked.

My aunt had told me "everything" about her, but she refused to reveal her name despite my insistence, her excuse being that revealing it might spoil our first meeting. She would repeat that not mentioning her name ahead of time would make our first meeting seem more natural and spontaneous.

"Just show up to my house around sunset, the time she usually visits me," my aunt had said. "Without warning. Just like that. It will look like you were in the neighborhood and decided to come up and visit me. I'll introduce you two and insist that you stay and have coffee with us. This way I'd be truly mentioning her name for the first time, and I won't feel self-conscious or guilty."

"Why would you feel guilty?" I asked.

To this day, I still do not understand why she said that or why she would feel guilty for telling me her name. When I called my aunt recently, I reminded her of that incident. I insisted that she tell me the truth about my wife, and nothing but the truth, but she pretended that she did not remember that incident.

"What truth are you demanding to know, anyway?" she said. "You keep talking about the truth."

"She used to meet that French guy at your house before we got married," I said. "Why didn't you tell me about that?"

I was able to force some information out of her—that she had had them over once or twice and that they had sat in the living room. She said she never let them out of her sight except once, and it was only for five minutes, the time it took her to go down to the store to buy some coffee.

She said she had not told me about it before because there was nothing to tell. It had simply been a "meet and greet" type of rendezvous, in a safe and decent place.

No! It had definitely been more than that.

He was ten years younger than my wife, but her heart melted the instant he entered her life. Seemingly by pure coincidence, he had moved into the same building where my aunt lived, but actually she had met him before that. My aunt had met him on the street, also by pure coincidence, as he roamed around confused and struggling to construct an Arabic sentence about finding a hotel. He had been living in an expensive hotel in Hamra and wanted to find a new place. That was how my aunt ended up hosting him for two nights. During that time he left early in the morning and did not come back until late at night. That meant they saw him only rarely! He had offered my aunt some money for letting him stay for two days, but she told him it was a ridiculous offer and that she did not need the money. And then, with her help, he rented an apartment in the same building, for just a few months, which he paid for up front in cash. Of course, this impressed the landlord, who welcomed him warmly. Because unlike locals, who act as if they own the place once they start renting and never leave, foreigners are always in transit. And on top of all that, the landlord loved him and took him in just like my aunt had. But my wife could not visit him as often as they both would have liked because the neighbors' eyes were always watchful when it came to the whereabouts of a single woman visiting a single man who lived alone! As the neighbors' single daughter, my wife had to meet him at my aunt's house instead.

Things must have progressed between them, prompting her to start asking me to teach her the French terminology for intercourse—so she could communicate with him in his own refined language. And that was at the same time that Jospin, the socialist and humanitarian French prime minister, was calling the Lebanese "terrorists" for resisting Israeli occupation inside Lebanese territory. When I heard that, I was so upset I tried to kick his car through the TV, just as some college students from Birzet University in the West Bank were doing. I almost smashed my television screen.

My wife did not really need to learn that language since the language of the flesh is one, both unifying and unified, everywhere. It is born within us and stays alive. And besides, they could have communicated in English, which he knew, in addition to the little bit of standard Arabic and Lebanese dialect he had come to Beirut to learn. I guess he preferred her to talk to him in Arabic only, an enviable position for any language student to be in, but she must have made the correct decision that using French words at the right moments was more appropriate and would make the situation more enticing.

She would ask me to teach her those terms when we were in bed, during our most pleasurable moments. Out of the blue, she would ask me, "How do you say *that* in French?" The first time she asked me, I said, "What do you mean by *that*?" I was still inside and on top of her, so she lifted her pelvis a little and said, "*This.*" I did not understand what she was talking about, so she tried to clarify it. "In English they say that someone *came*," she said. I do not remember the exact word she used in English, but she wanted the French equivalent.

"*Jouir*," I said. "*J'ai joui.*"

"What about 'Did you come?'" she asked.

"*Tu as joui?*" I repeated a few times. "*Tu as joui?*"

I hesitated to ask her why she wanted to learn to say those things in French. I should have asked her. But if I had asked her, she would have gotten mad and turned her face as if I had committed an unforgivable crime, or as if I had accused her of the most hideous crime a loyal woman devoted to making her family happy could be accused of. Even the remotest and most indirect accusations would upset her. But one time, I could not stop myself from asking her why she wanted to learn French. I did not ask why she wanted to learn "those words" in particular because I did not want to upset her. I also told her she was the only one in those days who was going to war instead of coming back from one! What I meant was that most people were now learning English because it was the language in demand. She said that, first of all, she already knew English and that she loved French, which she found tender, gentle, profound, and cultured. She said she loved her French-speaking friends and wanted to be on par with them in their language and knowledge and high culture. Oh, my God. My wife sat up from where she was lying naked on the bed to tell me that. She sat up and covered her nakedness, gesturing right and left as she spoke. Language failed my wife as she tried to explain her deep and complex thoughts, so she had to resort to using her hands, the way hosts of cultural shows do when they are emulating the ways of intellectuals. They use their hands as if trying to unleash their innermost thoughts from hard-to-reach places.

Everything had progressed normally until the landlord smelled a rat and decided to take action. He kicked the French man out despite his attempts to put his foot down and despite his insistence that he had a right to privacy and independence as a human being with legally protected rights. But apparently my wife got involved and convinced him to disappear before things could escalate into a scandal and cause her some serious damage. That was when my aunt talked my wife into marrying me. That same aunt who used to tell me to live my life as I pleased without worrying about social propriety and who told me not to listen to people who advised me to hurry and get married before I got too much older.

When I called my aunt to ask her if she had heard what happened between my wife and me, she said that my wife's mother had told her about it but that she had not seen my wife or talked to her at all. She also said, "Don't take this lightly, especially when it comes to her brothers."

"Whose brothers?" I asked.

"The seamstress's brothers," she said.

While I was in the middle of talking to her, my doorbell started ringing relentlessly, so I had to get off the phone. I told her I'd call her back. Before we hung up she said, "Be careful. That might be her brother at the door." I didn't get a chance to ask whose brother she was talking about.

The relentless person at the door turned out in fact to be the seamstress's brother.

His belt buckle caught my attention. It was the kind of buckle that would never pass airport security, the kind of buckle a person could use to hijack a plane and threaten to kill the passengers with if his demands were not met. He came right in and headed directly to the dining room table. He loosened his belt by two notches as if he'd just eaten an entire sheep stuffed with rice cooked in pure fat.

"The authorities will be here shortly to take you to jail," he said.

I smiled like someone totally in control of the situation and said, "There's a procedure for these kinds of things. You'd have to press charges, and I'd have to tell my . . ."

"I could drop the charges right away," he interrupted. "I could agree to settle and it would be all over. For five thousand dollars!"

"No way," I said. "I did not assault your sister."

"Don't you dare mention my sister! And if you must, go wash your mouth out first!" Then he took his belt off faster than you can imagine and whipped it across my hands clasped in front of me on the table. That hurt so much, but with those two hands of mine that were aching with the worst possible pain, I managed to hit him in the face so hard it surprised even him. He would have fallen to the floor if he hadn't managed to catch himself with a sudden acrobatic move. He was younger than me but much bigger and taller. I took advantage of his momentary loss of balance and got a knife from the kitchen, which he immediately snatched from me. He slapped me in the face and said, "Shove it up your ass! But not now, in forty-eight hours!"

What precision!

Then he said, "And be careful not to cut your asshole when you're sticking it up there!"

He was such a stupid idiot.

He had given me forty-eight hours to come up with five thousand dollars to settle accounts and patch things up, and then he left.

Five thousand dollars! Was he kidding or what? Who did he think I was? Rafik al-Hariri? Bill Gates? Where did people like him learn to think in terms of such big numbers? It wasn't just currency that was inflating; everything was inflating, everywhere, our heads most of all. That night he called me himself, the damned extortionist, to advise me not to rely on my wife anymore because she had removed herself from the game by fixing things between them. "Your wife is very smart! A whole lot smarter than you!"

What did he mean by that?

So my wife must have gotten her uncle to help her, possibly by appealing to some candidate running for parliamentary elections who believed winning was determined by the number of votes you got and had agreed to mediate, hoping to get her and her uncle's votes along with anybody else who owed him some favors. Was she actually going to vote for him despite her professed lack of faith in elections in our part of the world? Would she even know to repay the courtesy? I don't think being gracious is one of my wife's habits. (She never thanked me when she found out she was pregnant!)

My wife had made up her mind to let the seamstress's brother come after me. (Did my aunt know?) My wife felt that was her right, especially if she was no longer associated with me. She was going to do as she pleased, and I was supposed take whatever she threw at me. I guess "it's okay," like my wife likes to say in these circumstances. She had hunkered down in a different trench. Fine. She was in one trench and I was in another. Whatever.

Fine! If I had to engage in that battle, then so be it. I would be triumphant in the end, God willing. Where was she going to run to, after all, with me inside her, in her belly, in her womb? The only escape from me would be death. Yes, death, nothing short of that.

Her belly would give her away! She could lie about everything else as much as she wanted, but she could not stop her belly from growing big and round. And she would not be able to wiggle out of her relationship with me either, which was going to surprise the seamstress's stupid lowlife brother. She was not going to be able to change the laws of nature, unless she had some amazing stroke of genius. God knows what that might be. The only brilliant ideas she ever had were for deception. She's weak and not very inventive, except when it comes to lying! She's capable of endless lies as long as her image remains pure and pristine.

She's a virgin! In body and soul. She was a virgin much more in soul than in body. My wife never takes the blame for anything that happens to her unless she is forced to. Even if she hid something from the one person who should know everything about her, because he is her husband after all, she claims it is because she is afraid of being misunderstood. However, she herself is supposedly virtuous and completely unattainable. When I had first met her at the Rawda Café she claimed she had not had any previous relationships. Only things that happen to every girl, she had said. But as it turned out, she had been engaged.

No, no, no, not formally engaged, but the young man visited her all the time.

"He was always coming over to our house."

His parents and her parents had been well aware of the fact that he was "always coming over." Their relationship had been taken for granted. The idea that they would eventually get married was never brought up. As she described it, she had been just a child who knew nothing about the ways of the world! Poor baby.

I knew nothing about any of it! If not for the bits and pieces she had given me, I never would have known.

No, no. That was something no one knew about because it did not actually happen, at least not the way things usually happen. The young man in question was an adolescent, a relative of hers. "He was my cousin!" she said. She nearly choked when she first told me.

Everyone around them thought they were just good friends, that there couldn't possibly be anything more going on between them. The older folks especially thought that because of the huge age difference between them—eight years.

"I was very young," she said.

Oh God!

"Don't blame my relatives," she used to say whenever I'd get all worked up and ready to fight.

"Take them all to court! Send them all to jail! That was child abuse, and the others were complicit!"

No! Not according to my wife! Because there hadn't been anything they did or didn't do for which they could be blamed.

She had also said that because she was so young, she must have had all sorts of illusions. Eventually her cousin got married. She was sixteen at the time and had been taken aback by the whole thing because, in her innocence, she hadn't expected that. And that's all there was to it.

How could that be all there was to it if she had nearly choked when she mentioned his name?

"Actually, I was so aggravated when he went to the Gulf and got married to some Syrian girl he met there and then sent his mother a picture of his new wife and wrote on it that she looked like me! My aunt showed me the picture and what was written on the back: "Doesn't she look a lot like my cousin?" I managed to read what he had written, but I couldn't bring myself to take a close look at the picture and see if she really looked like me or whether it was some kind of sick joke because my eyes were full of tears."

"That's how it made me feel," she said. "Like I'd been stabbed, because it confirmed that my feelings were based in reality."

"How so?" I asked her. "On the contrary, that should have confirmed that your feelings were baseless. It should have proved that everything you thought was real had been nothing but a fantasy. Most of all, it should have proved your cousin did not think of you as a woman. That to him you were just a relative, nothing more."

"How he thought of me was the least of my worries!" she shouted, furiously.

"It's ancient history," I told her. "It happened fourteen years ago. Why should it still upset you so much?"

She never answered that question, and she wouldn't answer my next pressing question about whether her cousin was now living nearby somewhere in Beirut either.

"Please, Auntie, I'm begging you," I pleaded. "Tell me if my wife's cousin returned from his travels. I beg you to tell me in all honesty what you know about her relationship with him."

"I know nothing about it," she replied. My aunt seemed surprised by the question. "Now, tell me, more importantly, what have you decided to do about the brother?" She advised me to come to some kind of agreement with him because the situation was scandalous no matter how you looked at it. She even offered to give me a thousand dollars. "You can have it. No one needs to know anything. It'll be our secret, forever. Go and end it right now, and make sure no one else gets involved. Take care of it before your mother finds out, because right now she only knows what I've told her, which is that you and your wife are having some problems and soon the dark cloud hanging over you will pass."

"Is her cousin here in town now? Has he come back from the Gulf?"

"I vaguely remember her mother mentioning about a week or so ago that he dropped by with his four daughters for a visit."

"When? At night? During the day? Was my wife there?"

"All I know is that he and his four daughters came by for a visit, and that his wife is pregnant again because he wanted a boy. But, they had an ultrasound recently and it's a girl."

I had learned from my wife that he had four daughters and no sons. She had said the reason he did not have any sons was because of a curse she had placed on him—that he would only have girls so he would appreciate their value and what it would feel like if they were treated lightly and without respect and consideration.

"What do you mean lightly?" I asked her. "From what you've told me, it doesn't sound like he treated you lightly at all. Unless you're hiding something from me. And, at this point, I'm almost certain you've been hiding many things from me—some major things in fact."

She said she had told me the whole story in brief. She had told me a condensed version of the whole story because it was an old story and she did not remember all the details anymore. I protested and told her that she had not forgotten anything at all because what had happened must have left a wound that was still fresh and bleeding.

In the end, because of my persistence, my wife could not keep hiding the truth. It became harder and harder for her to keep that secret etched in her heart and, no doubt, in my aunt's. She was forced to reveal something new about her story each time it was brought up, until one day she ended up telling me the entire story from A to Z.

They had been in the car, and her mother was driving while her aunt sat in the passenger seat. She was in the backseat, sitting on her cousin's lap, and her older sister and his younger sister were also in the backseat. She was nine, and he was sixteen. They were on their way to visit a strip of land in the South that had been turned into a tourist site after its liberation from the twenty-year Israeli occupation. They had agreed that on the way down her sister and cousin, her aunt's daughter, would sit on the side facing the sea, while she and her other cousin, her aunt's son, would sit on the side facing the mountains. They had planned to switch sides on the way back home.

Her mother and aunt were busy discussing the South, which they were about to visit for the first time since the first Israeli invasion. The atmosphere on the road was festive. Billboards praising the sacrifices of the resistance movement filled the streets, and private vehicles and public transport carried the masses and the diplomats. Busses transported schoolchildren from all over the country as well as from the rest of the Arab world. Her sister and aunt's daughter were preoccupied watching the beautiful coastline as they traveled past Beirut and Sidon, and my wife was on the verge of dozing off in her cousin's lap, as she always did whenever she was in a car on a long trip.

It was about nine in the morning when he slipped his hand between her thighs, touching her and inserting his finger inside of her. She was startled by what happened but didn't say anything. He kept on caressing her, and she felt strange sensations that she had never experienced before. She had no words to describe these sensations. She wanted to tell him to get his hands off her, but he was holding her tightly and affectionately, the way he had always done for a long time now, which she liked. Her most vivid memories of him were of him carrying and hugging her playfully. She would call him "my husband," which made everybody laugh—except for her dad, who once told her, "Don't say that!" She had been shocked and ran to her mother to tell her what happened. Her mother told her that her dad always assumed the worst in people and that she shouldn't worry about what he said.

Her cousin then put his mouth close to her ear and whispered, while nibbling on her ear, "Are you happy?"

She nodded in agreement. Somehow she was truly "happy." He said, "Don't you dare tell anybody!" Then he threatened her, "If I find out you told anybody, I will never marry you!" His words scared her. She was so scared and worried that she started to cry. When he saw her crying, he took his hand off of her, which made her worry even more that he was now upset and would leave her. "Keep your hand there," she said. "I'll keep it on one condition," he said, "That you promise me over and over again that you will never mention anything about this to anyone!" When she promised him that and swore on the lives of her father, mother, and siblings that she would keep her promise, he slipped his hand back inside her and started caressing her again, before suddenly pulling her forcefully, which hurt her.

And, so, that child grew up—that child who would one day become my wife, thanks to my aunt's conniving. She grew up, with the hope that he would marry her, on condition that she would not tell anybody about what had happened between the two of them for seven whole years.

So what had really happened between them?

My wife claimed and insisted that he never penetrated her, not even once! So, I kept telling myself, "Try and believe that, Rashoud! Good luck."

"How do you expect me to believe that?" I said to her many times. "What gives you the right to ask this of me? I just cannot do that."

I told her very sincerely that I wanted to believe that she had told me the whole truth, but I couldn't. From the bottom of my heart, I told her that I couldn't believe her, and I asked her for help.

"Help me!" I said. "I want to believe that you're not a liar. But you have to help me believe what you said."

"It's up to you to believe me or not," she would say sometimes. "You're a free man and an adult. You're not a child anymore. You're responsible for your beliefs and actions."

I didn't understand what she meant by that, and I couldn't tell whether she was mocking me, or what.

"How is it possible that you stayed with him for seven whole years, maybe more, and the two of you didn't go all the way, like any normal couple?"

"I didn't stay with him," she would say. "That was just the way things were, the natural course of things. In my innocence and naiveté, I thought of him as my future husband, that he would be mine when the right time came, and that I was his forever. I never discussed this with anyone, and I never thought about it. I didn't think about anything else that would refute that possibility either. Don't you get it? I had no idea what it meant to be husband and wife, the way we are now. Get it?"

"Yes, I get it," I said. "But tell me, what did you two do the entire seven years, since you didn't . . ."

"All you care about is *that*," she would say, as if reprimanding me.

She said it as if *that* was not important. I remember thinking: What then would you consider important—you, who are so liberated? You, the satellite TV addict? Tell me what could be more important than my wife's sexual adventures? My wife, who shares my bed and is the mother of my children, who carries my name and is linked to me by that name. If someone were to lay a hand on my wife, he'd be violating me too, in every sense of the word. She was my wife, and if another man has penetrated her, he's penetrated me too! (Oh, dear God!) And if . . .

According to her, he had been the one getting all the pleasure from her, while she never took any initiative—until she hit sixteen!

"So, how exactly had he been getting all that pleasure from you?" I asked. "Who else has the right to this information but your own husband, your husband who accepts you despite everything, his only condition being that you tell the truth? I sure hope that he didn't penetrate you and that you enjoyed it. I hope you were an innocent hostage and a victim of your naiveté and your parents' and relatives' ignorance. But you must tell me what happened in detail." I told her I wanted all the details. All of them. Nothing more, nothing less. In fact, I told her I'd rather know too much than too little.

They did not have any place where they could be alone. So they would meet at her parents' house when he came by with his mother for a visit, or vice versa, when her mother would bring her along to visit.

When she grew older, her aunt started noticing how well she and her cousin got along, and her aunt talked to her mother about it. She confided that she would love for them to end up together, to which the mother replied that it was all in God's hands. But she also added, "Why not?" The cousin, however, never told my wife anything. He never spoke to her of love or feelings or anything like that. He never promised her anything. It was she who had assumed that what was happening between them was quite normal and that they would get married sometime soon, when circumstances allowed. Not once did she doubt that. It was strange.

Whenever the two of them got together at one of their houses, they would go off into a room by themselves. He would sit beside her and kiss her, but they never undressed.

"Even when you were sixteen and he was twenty-four? Do you really expect me to believe what you're claiming, that in your whole life you've never seen another man besides me? You expect me to believe that's true? Is it possible that over the course of seven long years, through all those winters and all those summers, you never found yourselves all alone, unsupervised, for an hour or so, and you never got undressed even once?"

My wife claimed she had never seen a man's penis before. Why would she make such an unbelievable claim?

"I asked you right from the start, the very first time we met at the Rawda Café, to be honest with me because I was serious about you. You made me believe you were telling the truth, but you lied to me, and now we're both paying the price for that lie.

"So how come you bled, then? Where did the blood come from the night we had sex for the first time?"

"I did it for you! When you started pushing for us to get married, demanding that we do it right away, I went to see a doctor . . ."

"Male or female doctor?"

"What difference does it make?

"I asked him to do the surgery right away. That's where the blood you're asking about came from! I did that for your sake!" she finally admitted.

That was what she always said whenever the subject came up and she saw me getting upset. She would insist that she had had that operation for my sake, so our marriage would succeed.

"And when you told me what your friend's girlfriend said, I thought I'd done the right thing and that this was a gift you would highly value."

It's impossible to imagine a person more capable of twisting things to suit her whims than my wife.

My wife—the powerful! The almighty! The most cunning!

Rather than admitting she was a liar and a fallen woman with no morals, my wife had somehow managed to recast herself as having sacrificed for my sake!

Wow! How decent of her!

She was so in love with me she made huge sacrifices for my sake, one of which was stitching her torn hymen back together to make me think she was a virgin because I would never have agreed to marry a deflowered woman!

My wife found it so strange that I wouldn't marry a deflowered woman, like I'm some kind of bizarre creature no one's ever seen the likes of before. But, because she loved me so much, she had accepted me like something that couldn't be avoided, and she had sacrificed for my sake, put her health at risk, and undergone surgery in order to make her body whole again, exactly the way I wanted it. Then she had hid all that from me so I wouldn't worry or suspect anything!

Yes, that's right!

It didn't take great intelligence on my part, though, to lead her into confessing all those weighty matters she had hidden from me. She gave herself away all by herself, without realizing it and without my making the slightest effort. At the mere mention of her aunt's name, my wife turned red and green and yellow. One time, when she found out that her aunt had dropped by her mother's for a visit, she threw a fit—not because she had visited her, but because her aunt didn't call ahead to ask her mother if it was okay and to let her know she was coming.

"It's either me or my aunt!" she would threaten her mother.

She never wanted to be in the same place with her aunt, especially not at her parents' house, which was why she insisted that her mother should make the aunt call before coming over, so she—my wife—could avoid being there. When my wife heard that her cousin had gotten married, she became irate and divulged all her secrets. She told her mother about everything she had been expecting from her cousin, and she told her, as irrefutable proof of her claims, that he had taken her virginity at the tender age of nine. That ignited a war that raged between the mother and the aunt for some time. They eventually made peace after the aunt offered to do whatever she could to help, including promising to persuade her son—if what my wife was claiming was true—to pay for her travel to France or England to have the hymen restoration operation there. But my wife refused adamantly. She stomped her feet on the floor and hollered: "I will take care of myself!"

During this whole mess, I was a model of cooperation and love—and tolerance—despite the severity of the situation. I came up with the perfect solution to deliver us both from the daily torture we had been living through. After a lengthy discussion and days and nights of give-and-take, she finally agreed to go together to see a gynecologist and ask her to determine whether my wife had lost her virginity a long time ago, whether it had been by someone's finger, or if it had happened recently by something other than a finger. Based on what the doctor said, we would decide who was right and who was wrong, and from there each of us could make a decision that suited him or her. If she really had been violated by being fondled down there at a young age, then I was prepared to forgive her completely and end the matter right there. I would forget it altogether, as if it had never happened. I am not some murderer, or jailer or executioner. I am just a simple man asking that life give me the minimum: a virgin. I must admit that her agreeing to go with me to a doctor of my choosing to get some expert advice on that topic in particular was a step on her part which I appreciated very much. It was another bit of proof of her good intentions and willingness to get along and live in harmony.

As for what would happen if it turned out otherwise and the loss of her virginity was much more recent—well that was a different story. My decision in that case would be crystal clear, no questions whatsoever. If that was the case, there was no way I was going to let her play games and humiliate me like that. I would make her pay the price. There were certain things about her position on the matter that made me suspect this might be the case, one of which was her claim that the doctor would not be able to tell if her virginity had been taken by a finger or by the other thing. My response to that was that we should just listen to what the doctor was going to say first before drawing our own conclusions. There was no point in getting ahead of ourselves.

Another thing that raised my doubts was her insistence on going to see her own doctor. I flat out refused that idea because I thought he might back her up or conspire with her—especially with his experience as a gynecologist, which would have taught him to be an advocate for women after seeing with his own eyes the kind of torture they suffered. Personally, I do not like women to go to male doctors unless there is some kind of an emergency. Otherwise, they should just go to a female doctor. I do not like male gynecologists. They seem to me like they do not belong there. As a man, I have always believed that there should be certain things about my wife that are only for me, things I do not want to share with anyone. Not by touching or seeing or smelling. I mean, I am not narrow-minded, but I want there to be one woman in the world who is all mine and mine alone. What is so surprising about that? I cannot take pleasure in a spot someone has gotten to before me. I go for days feeling too irritated to go near something the doctor's had his hands on. Who could blame me for feeling that way, and why? That is the way my brain works. I am not saying a woman should avoid seeing a male doctor no matter what, not at all. All I am saying is that if there is a female doctor available, a woman should go to her. Is that narrow-minded? What is narrow-minded about it? When the doctor's eyes fall upon the thing about my wife that turns me on, for me it is like he has stripped me naked, disgraced me, and shamed me. How much worse if he was to touch that spot and poke around down there? How can you ask a person to be turned on by the body, by particular special parts of it, and at the same time allow that body to become public property? No way!

I cannot stand those pretentious, snobby poets who take pleasure in hearing themselves ramble on about women and women's liberation. Women are this and women are that. "A woman is like a beautiful book," one of those popular poets says. "Just because others have already enjoyed reading it, it shouldn't stop you!" No way! A woman is not a beautiful book! That is a bunch of nonsense, empty words. The only beauty in those words is the way they are expressed. If you only saw those poets and the way they really treat women!

I once heard a young poet say, "This one, I smell the scent of men on her." He waved the banner of modern poetry and refused to settle down in the older classical camp. A champion of modern poetry, he insisted on charging at the monuments of classical poetry to demolish them or whatever remained of them. He was not going to sleep for one second or lay down his arms until he had toppled the very last of those monuments.

"Hello, Bonjour Madame. One moment please," was the secretary's response when we called to set an appointment with the female gynecologist I had found. I had asked around about her morals from people who previously dealt with her, and they had recommended her.

A moment later, the secretary was back on the line. She gave us an appointment for the following week at ten sharp.

The following week?

A week was a long time for me, and I did not like that at all. Doctors often claim they are busy for the sake of publicity, which is why they set appointments days and days in advance or even schedule all their appointments at the same time to give the impression that clients come from everywhere to seek them out—making you believe that you too have to rush for a doctor's consultation! Was she one of those doctors?

That's too bad, I thought.

The day before our appointment, when my wife was not home, I called the clinic and asked to speak directly with the doctor after

introducing myself to the secretary. I told the doctor that all I
wanted from her the next day was for her to be honest and not hide
anything from me. I told her it was my one and only request. She
did not comment, but said simply, "Don't worry."

I decided not to rule out the possibility that that woman was
going to be honest. Perhaps it was true that she would not be
available until a week later. My experience with her eventually did
demonstrate that she was indeed honest, just as I had hoped.

She asked me to come into the examination room with my wife,
and she spent quite some time deliberating before giving her verdict.
She examined my wife thoroughly and consulted some books from
which she read some sections and studied colorful figures. Then she
called someone and talked to him using jargon I did not understand
at all. Then she asked us to have a seat at her desk.

She said, "Penetration occurred a while back, but I can't
pinpoint exactly when. Restoration of the hymen and its renewed
tearing must have occurred in the past few weeks, not before." I
asked her if she could estimate roughly when the initial penetration
had happened since she couldn't be precise.

"Was it a year ago? Two years? Three?" I asked.

"Not less than a few years ago," she said. "And I wouldn't be
surprised if it happened ten years ago, or even earlier."

I asked, "Could you tell the means by which the penetration
occurred?"

She looked surprised by my question and then said, "No."

I persisted, "Well, could it have been a sharp object? Or a
finger, perhaps? Or maybe even something else?"

She said, "Frankly, I can't tell for sure. But it looks like it
happened without any tearing outside the canal."

Then I asked her, "Can you specify the size of the thing by
which the penetration happened, I mean, its girth?"

She seemed annoyed by my question, but I did not back down. I
explained to her that I had come specifically for that purpose, to get
the whole truth, and for no other reason. I said my wife was not sick,
thank God, and there was nothing shameful about wanting the truth,
especially when it came to matters that fell along ethical and religious
lines. My remaining questions were focused on finding out whether

prior to getting married my wife had had intercourse regularly or intermittently, starting when and until when. She could not give me any definite answers. "But," she said, "I can say with absolute certainty that she has not had a baby or an abortion. As to whether or not she'd had sexual intercourse, you either believe her or you don't."

"What's your advice on this?" I asked. "Should I believe her or not?"

She shrugged her shoulders, a sign that she could not offer any help with that. Then she said, "She's your wife, and this is between the two of you. I shouldn't interfere in this matter, nor do I want to."

Trying to clarify what I meant, I said, "Here's what I want to know. Now that you've examined her and seen everything with your own eyes, are you inclined to think that she was in a regular or sporadic sexual relationship or none? That's what I meant to say."

She asked me how long we had been married, and I told her for a month. I understood what she was getting at with that question, so I added, "But we've only had actual intercourse ten times."

She smiled slightly, indicating that she had picked up on the fact I was counting the times I slept with my wife.

That had been the outcome of our doctor's visit. We had not made any progress.

My wife was silent the whole time, as if she had been transported to another world and had no connection to the place where we were. Her eyes were damp as if she was on the verge of tears, as if she was looking but not seeing anything.

We did not exchange even one word after leaving the doctor's office. It was as if I had just come out of the sea, after nearly drowning and being rescued at the last moment. I had no energy whatsoever in that hot and humid coastal city—Beirut in August. The temperature was above average and the power was out because of a shortage in fuel needed to operate the electric generators. The supply companies were complaining that the electric companies were not paying their mounting bills. My wife and I went our separate ways. But I was able to tell her, as I headed in the opposite direction, "I'm going to find out how much a TV costs."

I did not find out how much a TV cost, but I did think that I had made a mistake in my marriage. In fact, I thought I was destined to suffer. I was a plaything in the hands of fate, which God Almighty sometimes allows to play with people's destinies—some people's destinies. Perhaps demons were toying with me. They must have found a weakness and were using it to control me.

Yes, it must have been demons!

Don't demons exist? Could anybody really deny their presence?

How else could this be happening to me? I never thought in a million years that I could become a victim of this sort of thing.

I remember reading the *Thousand and One Nights* for the first time. I was still on the verge of my youth. I was shocked and disturbed because throughout my adolescence, I had dreamed of becoming a king since I loved women so much. In my mind, the king possessed as many women as he wanted, and women dreamed of being possessed by him. They all dreamed of being loyal to their husband the king.

"I am the king!" I wrote in my books and notebooks, as well as on the blackboard in class. Today, when I turn the pages of the books I kept from that time in my life, I am amazed by that urge, or rather that obsession. Even my friends called me "I am the king," which infuriated me, because I wanted them to call me "the king." I wanted them to say, "The king has arrived," and "The king has left," not "'I am the king' has arrived" and "'I am the king' has left." But there was no way that I could take back their nickname for me, and I felt brutalized every time I tried.

How could those women betray their husbands, the kings? The first pages of the *Thousand and One Nights* were like a slap in my face! A woman betrays her husband with slaves out in the wilderness:

Shahzaman, Shahrayar's brother, watched. Suddenly, the gate opened, and there emerged from it twenty slave-girls and twenty slave-men. His brother's wife strutted among them. She was a picture of beauty and grace. They walked until they reached a clearing, where they took off their clothes and sat with each other. Then the king's wife said, "Masoud, Masoud." And a black slave came to her, and the two of them embraced. Then he made love to her, and the rest of the slaves did the same.

It was as if someone had placed a stick of dynamite in my brain and lit the fuse! To borrow a metaphor from my wife and her mother, I was like a truck that had lost its brakes going downhill in a residential neighborhood crowded with children. What made the shock even more stunning was that such a beautiful, tender, ethereal, and pure creature—a woman—could sway the will of demons, which are far more superior to kings in their power and tricks and cunning! These women did not use their superiority for the sake of good, but for the sake of evil. These women did not outsmart the demons simply to be freed from their grasp. No, they avenged themselves by having sex with other men.

"I wish to see [it . . .] with my own eyes," said King Shahrayar to his brother Shahzaman. And when King Shahrayar bore witness to that horrible spectacle, he lost his mind completely. "Come, let us go from here," he said to his brother Shahzaman. "Kingship means nothing to us now. Let us travel far and wide searching for another who has suffered such a blow as ours, and if we fail to find such a one, then it would be better for us to die than live this wretched life."[. . .] Then suddenly a jinni appeared from the sea [. . .] balancing a heavy chest upon his head. He came ashore and settled down beside the tree from which the two men were watching. The jinni opened the chest and brought forth a large box that he also opened. Out from the box came a beautiful young woman, splendid as the shining sun. The jinni looked at her and said, "O Silken Queen, whom I have stolen from her bridegroom on her wedding night, allow me to sleep a while." He laid his head upon her lap and swiftly fell asleep. The young woman, having spotted the two kings up in the tree, lifted the jinni's head off her lap and gently lowered it to the ground. She stood up and, signaling to them, she said, "Come down from there. Do not be afraid of this demon." And so the two kings descended and the woman rose and stood before them. She reached into her pocket and pulled out a sack, and from the sack she pulled out a necklace made of five hundred and seventy rings. "Do you know what these are?" she asked the two kings, to which they replied that they knew not. "The owners of all of these rings had their way with me when this demon was not paying attention. Give me your rings as well." Without delay, the two kings proceeded to remove the rings from their fingers and give them to the woman. "This demon kidnapped me on my wedding night and placed me inside a box and placed the box inside a chest and sealed the chest shut with seven padlocks and threw me to the bottom of the raging sea with all its crashing waves. But what he did not know is that when one of us women desires something, nothing can stand in her way."

My whole reason for dreaming of being a king had been my desire to have all the women I wanted, and for them to belong to me and me alone. If a woman could betray her husband the king, then there was not a husband in the world whose wife would not betray him.

What a disaster!

Even if I were a king—and there was not much indication out on the horizon that I was going to become a king anyway—my wife might still betray me.

Whenever I would see a woman betray her husband in the movies, I always imagined her betraying him with me or for my sake. I liked that and felt relieved by that thought. All the women in the movies, whether single or married, were my women. I could take or leave any one of them whenever I wanted. Not a single one ever held back her desire for me, and they knew what I wanted without the least bit of effort, with a single gesture. They would understand me before I even got the words out, without any need to explain further. It would give me such consummate pleasure to read or hear that during the showing of some movie or another an actress came off the screen and appeared before her audience. That kind of thing would fire up my imagination, because it meant that the idea was out there and that people thought about it, which meant it could actually happen, even if the whole thing did start out as a fantasy. If an actress were to come off the screen and enter my movie theater one day, she

would certainly come directly to me. And she would be very happy
to meet me and get to know me and enjoy everything else that would
follow. All women were pure except with me, which was something
very nice and did not take away from their honor or character. For
thirty-five years I slept peacefully, rocked by that dream like a baby,
and now suddenly I was shocked to discover that my wife—who was
mine legally, truthfully, rightfully, realistically, and however you
want—was not really mine, and consequently, neither were any of
the others! Suddenly I discovered that the woman who was supposed
to belong to me had mixed her blood with a lot of other blood.

My dear little unborn child, in what kind of womb are you
growing? God cleanse you from all disgrace!

And on top of all this, just to kill you once and for all, she
claims she is pure.

She claims she is pure! She has never seen a man's penis before,
never touched one, never seen semen. So she claims, but then at
just the right moment, she knew when to push it away! Yes, she had
pushed it away to avoid getting spurted. And at the same time, she
hated intercourse and often said she wished a woman could get
pregnant without having to participate in that compulsory exercise.
Whenever I wanted to make love to her, that was what she would say,
trying to dissuade me, but if I insisted and she realized she could
not escape, she would connive her way out of it by pleasuring me
with her hand, without removing a single article of clothing.

If she did not love me, then why did she marry me? Maybe she
hated me the way her mother hated her own husband. She was her
mother's daughter after all!

Oh my God!

That mother of hers, that old, decrepit, seventy-plus-year-old
lady, who could not stand anyone who was not the famous Lebanese
singer Sabah or the likes of Sabah, like the actress Nidal al-Ashqar
or the writer Hanan al-Shaykh. That meant something.

That really meant something! Like mother like daughter. I used
to make fun of people who avoided marrying a girl whose mother
was not highly respected, but as it turns out, proverbs and wise
sayings do not come from nowhere. Unfortunately, we discover the
truth after it is too late.

It was not Sabah's songs that were shameful. I like her songs,
too. The shameful thing was the way my wife's mother went wild
when she heard those songs.

Sabah had been married and divorced numerous times, and
at nearly eighty she was married to a man her grandson's age.
Her previous husbands had come from every religion, sect, and
nationality under the sun. To put it simply and clearly, she was my
mother-in-law's idol.

The old lady would start getting ready early in the day for
watching Sabah in the evening on television and listening to
her sing. That was intriguing to me. And her husband would
be asleep. God forbid something happened to him during that
time. If the man had died she would not have even noticed. No
one would have known. One time she told him, "Don't you dare
complain about anything tonight. Consider me absent! Pretend I
am not even here!" And one time, while she was watching Sabah,
he started coughing out of control, and she did not bother to go
check on him.

That was just too much.

That kind of adolescent excitement at her age was really
frightening and unacceptable. It seriously gave one pause, especially
since the matter was not restricted to her adoration of Sabah, but
was an innate characteristic of hers that made her adore any woman
who was unconventional in some way or another. For example, she
loved Nidal al-Ashqar, the actor and producer, even though she
had never stepped foot in a theater. She loved Nidal al-Ashqar and
followed her news religiously because, in her words, Nidal was "a
strong personality!" In public and on television Nidal conducts
herself in a manner that is the envy of even the most powerful men.
"And she's a wife and mother, too!" my mother-in-law would say in
response to anyone who criticized her.

There was also that time when the novelist Hanan al-Shaykh
appeared on television and made public her affair with Ihsan Abd
al-Qudus. Hanan al-Shaykh was less than twenty years old at the
time and unmarried, while Ihsan Abd al-Qudus was around forty-
five, married, and had children on top of everything else. When
my mother-in-law heard that, she went absolutely crazy, so crazy

she could not sit still. She even knocked over a cup of tea without noticing what she had done. The daughter went about wiping the floor and picking up the pieces of broken glass while the mother got swept away with delight listening to that story.

It made one miss hearing stories about Sabah! At least Sabah's drama ended with marriage. Hanan al-Shaykh just went around falling in love for the sake of love.

Art for art's sake! That was what my mother-in-law favored above all else, and in addition to her fine taste, she only associated with women who were "bohemian." The women upon whom my mother-in-law bestowed this label were the ones surrounded with all the hush-hush, like her neighbor from the building across the street. My mother-in-law adored that woman. Her whole face would light up whenever she saw her or met with her. Rumor had it that this neighbor woman had an illegitimate child who was thirty now and working as an engineer in the Gulf. Supposedly, the boy's real father—the lover, in other words—paid for his education. I really did not know if my mother-in-law ever actually discussed these things with the neighbor woman, but there was no doubt whatsoever that she adored her and was always overjoyed to see her because of all the rumors.

"No, don't go yet. It's still early," she would say to her if she started to get up to leave, even if it was nearly dinnertime and she had not started preparing anything yet. She would also invite her to stay for dinner, the invitation coming from the bottom of her heart. She would be brokenhearted and filled with feelings of emptiness and melancholy when the woman left!

Yes, my wife had to inherit her lack of morals from somewhere. Her vulgarity had not come from a vacuum.

Our first time together, after I kept pestering her, she said to me, "Okay, fine. Come let me give you an oil change." As if I was a car engine or something! Can you imagine a bride saying such a thing to her husband? I guess she was just trying to be the kind of woman her mother admired—one with a strong personality.

When she sensed that I was about to reach orgasm, she pushed the head of my penis away from her face, in the opposite direction. Her preventive measures took me by surprise. In all honesty, I was so shocked I could not help but express how I felt, though I did it in a calm and innocent manner. I told her jokingly, "You seem like an expert at prevention." When she looked at me puzzled, I smiled, almost breaking into laughter, to make sure she took it only as a joke and did not think there was any ulterior motive to what I was about to say. I said, "You really are an expert at avoiding these kinds of situations!" As usual, she looked in the other direction and said with unwarranted defensiveness, "Living with you is hard." I told her that kind of talk was uncalled for and that I was just being playful. She said, "What kind of playfulness is that, really? You're a jealous man, and I can't live with a person who is so suspicious!"

"So suspicious?" How suspicious? And, on what basis was she saying that I was suspicious? Should it even be considered suspicion for a man to want to know his wife fully? I decided to deal with this matter with calmness and patience, telling myself that perhaps this woman was just oversensitive when it came to certain issues and that even though I had known her for a few months, I had not discovered or learned everything about her. "Man, you have to deal with these things with utmost calmness," I told myself. "In the end, she's your wife, and you have responsibilities toward her as much as she does toward you." I also told myself that she too must understand that.

I thought to myself back then that it was strange that she automatically understood exactly what I meant, even the things I did not know I thought or meant, because they were unimaginable to my mind. I wondered how she could have picked up on the fact that, at the most decisive moment, I noticed her moving my penis away to prevent my semen from getting on her clothes. She had also read my mind as I sat there wondering about how she knew that a man's semen comes out with such force and shoots so far. Only someone with experience would know that! I was convinced of that and nothing could dissuade me. I knew she must be used to having sex without leaving any trace of it on herself. She was used to having safe sex and was an expert at having intercourse without leaving any stains. She was like many other women, and by that I mean our women, not Meryl Streep and her kind. Those women are not in the business of being discreet or hiding anything, and that is their business, not ours. As our saying goes, "Every nation wears its own attire." My wife was like any other woman here—I mean some single women, who refuse to deprive themselves of life's pleasures, so they perfect the art of having sex without leaving a trace on their bodies or their clothes. When a woman here has intercourse with a man, she does not usually spend the night at his place because she cannot, so she does not have enough time to wash her clothes. She does not even take a shower at his place because a woman simply does not take a shower outside her own home—unless she is the devil himself! That is why they always resort to that clean and safe way of having intercourse.

And no matter how much a woman loves a man, she prefers not to dirty her clothes with his semen so he does not see any of its traces on her with his own eyes. Because if she sees him looking at her that way, it would be harder for her to deny that any of this happened later on, if the need arises. And, for this kind of woman, the need does arise quite often.

I wanted to confirm that my wife was no different from other single women in this matter—I mean those women who do it from behind to avoid being incriminated—but I was helpless. I was thinking that if she really did not allow her cousin to have his way with her, then perhaps she may have let him take her from the safer route, where there would not be the worry of getting pregnant and all its complications, and where she would never have to confess to intercourse or to undergo a hymen restoration later on. In the end, anal sex may be something that one could keep quiet about without feeling too guilty.

She cried the first time I tried to have sex with her that way even though I only prodded her fleetingly. I was relieved by her crying. I thought her crying revealed her feminine sense of shyness, that it was a positive sign. And I was not oppressive with her. On the contrary, all I wanted was to believe everything she said or felt. That was my dream. She was my woman, after all, my wife, my fate. One time, when I had surprised her by entering her a little from behind, she told me that she felt like going to the bathroom. How romantic!

One time, an Arab socialite was asked in an interview conducted by an Arab journalist if her sexual relationship with her husband was laid-back. She said very casually and without any hesitation that when she is with her husband at the right time and place, she doesn't feel any taboos whatsoever and that her husband can have her wherever he wants, however he wants, and whenever he wants. She smiled as she said these words—according to the journalist's parenthetical note. He added that she had smiled because her words were reminiscent of some famous lines by an attractive and sexy young woman from a commercial that appeared on Lebanese TV. It was a commercial for a cable company, and the gist of the ad was that the company was ready to connect any interested viewers with the best Arabic and international channels through cable, wherever their place of residence may be. The young woman in the commercial would say these words with a flirtatious Lebanese accent: "Wherever you want, however you want, whenever you want." And she would sit, stand, or lie down with every phrase she said, in a way that suggested that she was referring to herself, with her sexy body and bewitching charm.

Then the Arab lady courageously said, in response to a question the journalist used to try to outsmart and embarrass her, "Do you mean from behind? Why not? That's something I got used to in my single days, like many of our single women! I got so used to it, I started to love it. So why wouldn't I still like it now that I'm married?"

Was this socialite really so different from my wife, who read nothing but that kind of news in magazines, and in two languages, Arabic and English? Not to mention the shows and movies on cable TV.

I assumed that if I could confirm that she had had sex that way, she would be in serious trouble for lying about it and all her proclamations of purity and moderation would be exposed.

"What do you think I am," she said with agitation one day, "a whore?"

I decided to find out the truth in my own way. I wanted to find out if that back road had been "treaded," to borrow a village term; if someone else had been there before. I wanted to take her by surprise, crushing all her defenses, because a girl is under the impression that once her husband has confirmed her virginity, he will forget about everything else. She was right about that, but I was going to surprise her.

I waited for the right opportunity to examine that area, not only through touch, but also with my eyes and nose, and—why not?—through taste. But my mission was not easy because as soon as she would notice my attention drift to that area, she would become fully alert. I had made my decision and there was nothing in the world that would stop me from acting on it.

Like many people, I knew that exhausted parents sometimes gave their toddlers harmless doses of sleeping aid, so that for once they could do their thing and maybe get some sleep of their own. I put that same substance that parents put in baby bottles in my wife's cold beer, which she gulped down and thanked me for. She felt sleepy and went to bed. I followed her to the bedroom. As she lay there in bed, I told her I was going to take care of her that night, until she fell asleep. She told me to do whatever I wanted on condition that I let her sleep. That condition had a profound underlying meaning. Asking me to let her go to sleep meant not forcing her to get up to take a shower. What she had said basically meant: "Don't get me dirty." There was also the innocent, straightforward meaning, which was to simply not wake her up since she was tired. Incidentally, my wife loved it when I took care of her by caressing or massaging her with oils. She once told me, "I wish you were my masseur" (that is, not my husband), and I often baited her with these gestures, just so I could get what I wanted.

My wife nodded off like a baby and fell into a deep sleep. I immediately began caressing her in my usual way, starting with a little back massage, then on to the rest of her body all the way to her toes. (This usually put her to sleep even without a sedative.) Next, I concentrated on carrying out my main mission. The only light in the room came from the streetlights outside, so it was a bit dark, but there was a nice ambience and no need for additional lighting. Details were difficult to see, though, so I grabbed a little flashlight—one of those handy ones no household can do without around here since the electricity is constantly going out all of a sudden. I shined it on the area in question. It was impeccable. Not a single hair or the tiniest bit of fuzz, as if it was a forehead or a cheek or a lip! Now why would that be? The kind of care afforded to that area indicated it was most certainly a target for some special visitors my wife wanted to show around. I applied some lubricant and pushed my way in.

What ease! And she did not yelp, she did not wince, she did not *99* moan, she did not anything! Oh God. It was an open highway! I had not needed my lubricant!

So what did that mean? My God, what a despicable, cruel world.

Strangely, however, rather than acting on my rage and bashing her brains out, I found that I was absolutely incapable of removing myself from that spot. Contrary to what I would have expected, I felt an intense and rare kind of pleasure that hit me like a whirlwind. It was like those rare moments when I felt that she was all mine, that she belonged to me. I came inside her. I flooded her with semen that gushed forth from the deepest and outermost reaches of my being, from places that had remained neutral in the past. I simply could not resist that pleasure; it was many, many times more powerful than me. Even if my life were being threatened, even if I were doomed to a certain death, there was no way I was going to pull myself out of there and no way I was going to shoot my semen into the air, into nowhere, or onto a towel or onto the sheets, or onto a Kleenex with a prize ticket inside it, like the kind she was always yelling at me for throwing away. (How often I purposely wiped myself with those. I dreaded the possibility of her winning that car.)

I came inside her and I did not regret it.

Of course the fallout came the next day, when she woke up at around nine o'clock, a good two hours after me—two hours in which I wrestled over what I should do. I wondered if I should wait at home and face her anger head-on, in the event that when she got up she noticed some traces of the night before, or if I should leave and come back after she had a chance to calm down? Either way, I had to account for what I had done. And either way, there was no escaping her fury.

So let her get angry! So what? Was I not the man, after all? Did I not have the right to enjoy my woman whatever time of day or night I wanted, in whichever part of her I wanted? After all, it was not as if I had caused her any pain—she did not feel any pain there! It was not as if she was new to my coming there, or in her mouth for that matter! Did a stranger have more of a right to her than me? Did a stranger who was not her husband have more of a right to enjoy her in the place her husband was not allowed to go? That just was not right. It was absolutely intolerable.

The logical thing would have been to make her provide a full account! How and with whom and whether or not she used to be one of those women who practiced the safe sex method!

I decided to stay at home and wait for her to wake up and discover the traces of the events from the night before. The blood began racing through my veins when I remembered what my eyes had seen the night before, and I started connecting everything together in my mind. I heard her stirring, so I went to her in the bedroom. "I feel like I've been drugged," she said. Then she reached around and felt her rear and paused. I expected the battle to begin at that point, but she did not say anything. She tried to go back to sleep but finally got up and went to the bathroom. I tried to go in with her, even though I knew very well she would not put up with that, given her basic principle that the bathroom is a private place—an inviolably private place. But I was actually trying to cause trouble, because I could not just let it go so easily, without stopping there together to dot the i's and cross the t's. So I said to her, after hesitating for a long time over my opening remarks—which would be either a prelude to a discussion or to an argument—because if the conversation took a turn for the worse, it would not be my fault but hers. She was the one who was incapable of discussing anything that pertained to sensitive and essential issues concerning our marriage without crying and screaming in the end. So after some hesitation I said to her, "While you were sleeping last night, I filled you up so much it spilled over!" The moment the words came out of my mouth I realized what a vulgar and lowlife thing that was to say. I should have taken more time and been more patient choosing my words rather than tossing them out there like that. I should have told her something like what a beautiful time I had with her last night. I could have hinted about what I did by saying something like, "There isn't an inch of you that isn't as sweet as honey!" Or, "You're like a piece of fruit, tasty no matter where you take the first bite!" Instead, that horrible statement came out of my mouth all by itself, just slipped out involuntarily. I expected her to react with a violent storm capable of uprooting a ten-story building, so I braced myself and took all the necessary precautions, especially since I had already decided I should begin to make a retreat. Otherwise, things would stay unacceptably out of my control and against my will. Her reaction did not come as I had expected though. Actually, it was unimaginably worse. Her reaction was of a completely different nature—more like a car bomb packed to the hilt with atomic bombs and biological weapons.

And this is what she said:

"Well I hope you liked the smell."

Oh my God!

Did a more vulgar woman exist in this world? A more venomous woman? Could a human being possibly be any more despicable?

Her vulgarity and depravity were immeasurable. She was indeed an evil woman. Despite that, however, and based upon my undying belief in the importance of marriage and that we should not treat it like some old shirt we toss aside when we get bored of wearing it, I told myself that I should take things calmly and with an open heart. I should have some compassion. She was my wife after all, in spite of everything, and I was her husband. She was my garment, my bed, the dwelling place of all my desire. I thought of an answer that would not provoke her further, something that might push the conversation to a more favorable conclusion, because ultimately, that was what I wanted most of all. I wanted to know, once and for all, exactly what kind of being I was dealing with, what kind of person I was joined to from now until the end of time. I wanted to know what had been hidden from me, out of fear or shame. For so long, I had not been able to sleep at night worrying I might run into some man who had known her as I had known her or possibly more, and I worried he would know about me even though I did not know about him and he would be laughing at me secretly, mocking me, and feeling superior to me because basically he had refused to marry the woman I had been proud of marrying. But then again, why would he have refused to marry her after living with her like man and wife or something along those lines? Precisely because he had had her that way, and because she had let him have her that way, and because she had been easy, no matter how much she might have protested at first. That was why he had refused to marry her. A woman who allows a man to have her that way before getting married would allow any other man to do the same. What did that leave for her husband, the father of her children? I am a man, and I know how men think. That is how men think! It is the same logic that has controlled how I have behaved with girls my whole life. The very first time we met, I told her about such matters. I told her about all my experiences and encounters, in detail, so that my position would be perfectly clear to her. I purposely told her about how just the day before I had run into a woman I had slept with before, and after we got married, I told her again about running into her and how strangely she had acted. She was married and had two children. She turned red and looked around before greeting me, and not with a handshake for sure, because I did not extend my hand to her, and neither did she extend hers to me. She just kept smiling and practically laughing the whole time, which did not last more than two or three minutes. "I envy you," she had said. "You're still a bachelor without a care in the world! No children to burden you with responsibilities." She said that and gave a nervous laugh that sounded like a cough. After a little while we both relaxed a bit, and there was a nice chemistry flowing between us. "Do you have any regrets?" I asked her, and when she answered, "No, but . . . ," I did not let her finish. Instead I asked her, "Aren't you happy with your husband?" "Of course I am, but . . . ," she answered, and here I said, "If we'd gotten married, do you think you would have been better off?" I was hoping to establish a secret bond between us behind her husband's back, like a prelude of sorts for a little extramarital affair. The woman's face turned red, then green, then yellow, and one color after another. She burst into tears and said, choking on her words, "You think you're better than my husband?" I looked left and right to make sure no one was around, and as I walked away I said, "No. No. That's not what I meant. I was just saying . . ."

"Why did you say that to her?" my wife had asked. "Did you mean to offer yourself like a safety blanket she could wrap around herself whenever she got sick of her intolerable husband or her kids? Yes, they're a big responsibility, not easy to handle, especially for sensitive, selfless people who would give up everything they had and more for the sake of their children. I guess you were consoling her then." She added, "You're such a nice man, aren't you? You're so deeply in tune with mothers and their suffering."

After I had made sure that I was at a safe distance from the woman and that she was out of my sight, I wondered why she had burst out in anger like that, especially since she seemed so happy to see me, as evidenced by her smile, which reflected her true feelings. I also wondered what she really meant by "you think you're better than my husband?" Did she mean I was just as bad as he was, or that he was, in fact, better than me and that she was happy with him?

What I really wanted my wife to know about this story was its beginning and its beginning only. When I first met this woman, I felt she was attracted to me, and I felt something for her as well, but my feelings were not as strong as hers. It was a policy of mine to not get carried away with my feelings toward any woman so that they would not end up driving me places I did not want to go. We started meeting at coffee shops first with other friends and then alone. One day I invited her over to a friend's house. My friend had given me the key to his apartment and had left to give me some privacy, and she agreed to come over. So things happened between us, but, of course, they happened according to our cultural traditions, not like people do it in the West—or the movies produced there. She was, of course, a virgin, but we took off our clothes. She was so turned on that she was soaked in sweat. We spent a few minutes naked, rubbing up against each other. Then we would start all over again, which was normal. What was not normal, though, and what I did not expect, was for her to go straight to my penis and take it in her mouth, all on her own. Moments later, she started exhaling in a way that sounded like snorting. She had an orgasm while giving me a blow job. I was shocked.

People, you have to admit that a little coyness is more likely to fire up one's sense of anticipation and pleasure.

The very next day I went to the café only to find out she had gotten there first. She had put on her best clothes and was looking very sharp, as if it were her wedding day. She was dressed to kill. I ignored her and sat by myself at a different table, even though she was sitting all by herself at her table. Since that day—after getting married and having two children and despite running into each other every once in a while—she would not talk to me at all, not even say one word to me. She would not even greet me, let alone talk to me. It was as if she did not see me at all, even when it happened to be just the two of us somewhere, like in an elevator or at the same table. I must have stopped existing for her.

What my wife wanted to know was why I had decided not to sit with the woman on the following day. The reason was that I had gotten the impression that she had been in a "relationship" with one of the café's patrons, whom I did not respect or find worthy at all (not that it would have changed anything if I actually respected him), so I was worried that he would show up out of nowhere, see us together, and assume that there was something between me and her—especially with her being all dressed up like that. I was worried that he would assume that there was something serious going on between us and that he would treat me arrogantly based on his assumption that I was enjoying his "leftovers," or rather one of his "leftovers," since he had plenty of those.

My decision has not changed since then, but it is not really a decision anyway. It is something as natural as breathing, as natural as nature itself. And this is my decision: I will only marry a decent girl. By that I mean a normal girl, one without a scandalous history. Now, if I had to marry someone who had been in a previous relationship (and I say "a relationship," not "relationships"), one that was within reasonable boundaries, the girl would still have to be someone who did not run in the same circles I ran in. This way I would not have to come across the other man every day, especially since she might be with me.

No. That was not possible.

A friend of mine who teaches Arabic literature at a Beirut high school once said to me, after he had gotten engaged to one of his students, that "the most important thing for me was that she had not known a man before me, and that I was the first man in her life. How do you expect me to teach her the great poet Abu Tammam's lines about first love—that are part of the high school curriculum— and be her second or third or God knows which lover?" The lines go like this:

Go ahead, take your heart anywhere you want, in love.
There's no love truer than your first one.

A fellow may adore countless homes on earth,
But he'll forever long for his first home.

Now, I am not that strict. I realize that a woman is not merely created for the sake of the man she marries, and it is abusive to think otherwise. A woman is bound to meet different men in her life, and she might fall in love so deeply with a man to the point that it gets physical in some ways. That is very normal and I am not opposed to it. But that physical contact must be within boundaries. As for a woman taking a man's penis in her mouth without any prior notice or warning, now that is something I can neither accept nor tolerate. At the same time, I am not saying I should be imposing rules on a woman or punishing her in any way. She is free to do whatever she wants, but I am also free. I can understand why a woman would do something like that, once or twice or from time to time, upon a man's request or his stubborn insistence. But a woman who actually has the willful desire and inherent need to do it is just not my type personally. In fact, she is definitely nobody's type in our culture.

A man should receive his wife's body in perfect condition. It should be complete. It is a precious gift for a husband, one that will continue to affect him forever because it solidifies the bond between them as husband and wife, keeping this bond unbreakable. This way, the woman will have her head up at all times, never needing to hide her face, whenever talk about premarital chastity comes up. Her husband's respect toward her would be founded on conviction, not on pity or mere assumptions.

The first time I asked my wife to take me in her mouth, she said, "No!"

She did not say, "I don't like doing that." Her answer made me doubtful and suspicious, because, had she said, "I don't like that," I would have understood that she generally did not like doing that, ever, but in saying no her response remained vague because her no could mean that she refused doing that with me only. It is in these nuances that the meaning of things truly lies.

Days later, when I asked her again to do it and she said, "No," I did not ignore the situation the way I did the first time. I wanted to discuss it with her and find out why. It was my right. My intention in discussing it was not really to terrorize her. After all, I am one of those people who understand these things. I understand why a woman, even a wife, would refuse to be a man's slave in bed. That is very human, and I am not debating it. I would go as far as saying that when she refused to do what I asked her, I felt a deep sense of satisfaction. I like discretion in a woman, and that is a quality I know I have as well. What had really worried me was the fact that she said the word "no" twice, without elaborating on it. For instance, had she said something about not liking to perform that act in general or finding it downright unbearable, I would have completely understood. If she had said anything along those lines, I would have been reassured. But the fact that she did not say anything could have dangerous implications. After all, I was not an ignorant man when it came to these things specifically. I had read and heard that women do this thing with some men but not others. They might even choose to do it of their own free will with men who are not their husbands—and I am speaking from personal experience here— while not being able to really do it with their own husbands. And that is what blew my mind.

There was one thought I simply could not tolerate: that she had done it with some other man and so now she could not do it with me—her husband and the father of her children. I just could not deal with such a thing. No way. But maybe this petty, flat-out refusal of hers stemmed from a deep-seated matter of principle, which is why, the third time around, I forced her. Yes, I forced her, brutally, and without reservation, because one time at least, a man must prove to his woman that he is a man, especially if he can prove it without causing harm or pain and without leaving any marks or things of that nature. And furthermore, a man must thrust himself into his wife, into one of those spots she protects with such vigilance, so that she will feel her husband is a real man in every meaning of the word and that he is powerful and his might is justified and firmly established— and especially so she will feel she is his and that ultimately, to a certain extent, she is his possession. This is essentially what a woman longs for from her deepest depths. It is something she has a dire need for. God created man stronger than woman for a purpose, and that purpose manifests itself on precisely these occasions. Certainly God did not create anything haphazardly.

She resisted a lot before I forced her to do it. She tried to get away, but I had made up my mind and there was not a power in the world that could persuade me to bend my will. I was making a huge wager, worth sacrificing everything. Either she was going to take me in earnest as her husband, or she was going to stay the same—taking things lightly and not obeying me at all, sleeping at her parents' whenever she felt like it and spending all her time there without taking my wishes into consideration at all. Her anger reached its peak when I came before withdrawing from her mouth despite her wanting me to. She did not bite me because she was well aware I would hurt her badly if she lost her senses and committed such a disgraceful offense. Rather than doing that, though, she did something much more gruesome and much wilier. Right after all my strength seeped out of me after climaxing, she sprang up like a lunatic and pressed her mouth against mine, not to kiss me, but to feed me my own semen!

"Taste yourself!" she said.

Dear God. That whore, daughter of a whore, descendant of generations of whores!

In an attempt to get back at me, she had spit all of that fluid— that fluid God created for her to receive, like a holy receptacle—into my mouth. There are times when I think what is written in the old books about men and women is the truth! And nowadays we are too quick to dismiss those books and pass judgment mercilessly, without taking into consideration that those books were based on the fundamentals of how God created nature. For example, in one of those books it says the woman should not be on top of the man for the simple reason that, naturally, like any fluid, it flows downhill. Therefore, the best method for intercourse is for the man to get on top of the woman, after preparing a place for her to lie down and after lots of kissing and touching. The worst way is for the woman to be on top of the man and for him to have intercourse with her when he is lying on his back. It is completely against nature, out of which God created man and woman, or rather the male and the female. The woman is the one who has it done to her. If she starts being the one who does it, that goes against nature.

What a wonderfully simple and clear maxim!

There are certain things that remain stable and permanent no matter how much mankind advances and no matter how much the times change. The important thing is to get better at how we think about them, not just take them at face value. Respecting women is a duty. That goes without saying. A husband taking pleasure in his wife and a wife taking pleasure in her husband is also a matter that is not under dispute, but must stay within clear boundaries that anyone with eyes can see. If a man and a woman are harmonious, each has the right to enjoy whatever they like, whenever they like, however they like, and so on. But one must always remain vigilant of the boundaries so that even if they are not respected, a person can know how far from them, or close to them, he stands. No matter how much times might change or what new kinds of customs and traditions come about, a man is still a man and a woman a woman. A woman should always and forever respond to her husband when he calls on her, and she must obey him in decisive matters—even if that obedience is psychologically taxing for her—because she can easily be compensated for that obedience, as taxing as it may be, as soon as she sees her husband return to his forbearance, his mercy, and his virtue. And there is no question that he will return to that. But for her to leap up like a maniac in order to avenge herself by spitting what of him was in her mouth into his mouth, forcefully and spitefully, well that is just completely unacceptable.

When I took some of what was in her mouth into my mouth, I was shocked by its taste and smell. I did not feel dirty, but I felt something deeper than that, like having been despoiled, and I felt that I had been exposed to rape. So I spit out what was in my mouth at her and I pushed her away from me. She fell on the ground and seemed to be in pain. Then she got up and left the house, slamming the door behind her without telling me where she was going. But I knew, of course. Where else would she go in such a state? If not to that mother of hers who bore her in her own likeness. No one but her mother could listen to her and put her mind at ease and conspire with her. At any rate, her mother loved those kinds of stories in general. How much better if her own daughter was involved!

When I asked my wife once about that incredible love her mother felt for that friend of hers who made her so joyful, she said, "Birds of a feather flock together." I was surprised and made that clear to her. She responded briefly and wisely, "Nobody opened her heart to find out what was in it." But I answered her that there seemed to be tangible evidence. She said that nobody knows what is in a man's heart. Sometimes even what a man does will not reflect what is in his heart. I was surprised to hear that deep wisdom of hers. I did not know what to say. I did not say a word. I did not say a word because I felt in my own heart that by saying that, she was defending herself more than she was defending her mother or her mother's friend. It was her nature to take everything personally, as if it was directed at her or against her. For example, when I asked her once, before we got married, about this raving madness for Sabah, and I was specifically asking about her mother, she answered, "Stay out of my business."

I guess she adored Sabah, too. I did not know she liked her that much.

I do not claim to be a devout believer, and I know I do not have the right to judge people, but anyone with an iota of brains could not keep from making those connections and drawing those conclusions. On top of that, her mother does not pray, does not fast, and does not mention God's name. These qualities, when you put them together in an old woman—not a man—are a clear indication, a proof.

My wife and her mother looked very much alike. I say plainly that when she left me, I thought to myself—in spite of the pain I was suffering—that there was something positive in her leaving and divorcing me, which was that she would never grow old under my roof and would never start looking like her disgusting mother. That was something that weighed down on me, like a nightmare. I imagined her getting old and becoming just like her mother—as she is now—especially since the close resemblance between them makes it clear to anyone who sees them that they are mother and daughter.

This strong outward resemblance could only be a reflection of an internal resemblance, evidence of shared personality traits.

And the daughter's constant desire to stay at her mother's day and night proved it. Add to this the complete agreement between them, which manifested itself plainly when she left me: yet another solid proof. I can even go so far as to talk with a clear conscience about a conspiracy between the two of them, not just a mere agreement. Even now they are conspiring against me, like when I call to speak to my wife and her mother gives the nasty answer, "She's still out," or "She'll be back in half an hour." She tries to behave in a way that suggests she is neutral, that what goes on between me and her daughter is between the two of us, and yet in spite of that she is trying hard to help us mend our differences so that her daughter can go back to her husband. But one time when I called, she said right away that her daughter was at the beach. I was dumbfounded. When she realized that I had stopped talking, she was about to hang up on me, but I said to her, "Hold on a second." Then I said, "Does she have the right to take matters so lightly?"

"That's none of my business," she answered. "And even if I was willing to stop her from going to the beach, I wouldn't be able to. You know even better than I do how much she loves the beach, and you know that she kept up her habit even in the darkest days of the war when everything was difficult and prohibited. Don't you remember?"

"That's not what interests me," I said. "What I'm interested in is what's growing inside her womb." She did not say anything.

"Hello!"

"I hear you," she said. "What do you want me to say?"

It was strange the way her mother acted. A mother—any mother—would not normally remain silent when her daughter was having serious issues with her husband, like deserting her marital home, never mind being pregnant. She was the first one to know about the incident, since her daughter called her in tears and told her that she had missed her period and that I was an evil man. Meanwhile, I was so "smart" thinking she was so innocent.

"I want you to tell her that what's in her belly is not hers alone."

"..."

"Hello?"

"Yes, I can hear you. But what can I do?"

It was also strange that her mother did not interfere, not openly
at least, in the issue concerning my alleged rape of the seamstress.
She did not interfere either positively or negatively in that matter,
even though she was not normally a reserved person. In fact, she was
always sticking her nose in other people's business. She would always
interfere and take her daughter's side when I tried to persuade my
wife to go sleep at home. She would make up the most ridiculous
excuses to keep us at her place. She would say things like, "Oh, it's
getting late. You shouldn't leave now," or "This house is just so
scary without the kids around," and "Come on, there's a great show
on TV tonight. Why don't you just stay and watch it?"

Even my own mother had told me about one of her remarks.
My mother had started to catch on about what was happening so it
was impossible to keep things from her. My mother told me that my
mother-in-law had said: "Is a woman destined to go through all this
pain just to be with a man?" I completely believed that she would
say something like that because I knew from my personal experience
with her that she was not one of those women who believed that a
woman must have a husband no matter what the cost.

My mother-in-law must have regretted her marriage beyond
anyone's imagination. She even admitted that she was not very
attached to her husband. I heard her tell her best friend once that
her husband never took any initiative in bed and that when he got
into bed he would close his eyes and just let her do whatever she felt
like. "I married a little boy, not a man!" she said. She never felt that
he was a real man in any sense of the word. Yes, he may have been
an "adorable" person. He was undeniably kind-hearted, generous,
helpful, and a good friend—and possessed every good quality you
could ask for—but he was not a real man. She would always add:
"Women in our generation had to put up with so much!" She told
her without any shame, as she laughed like one of those whores in
cheap movies, that when he climaxed he would whimper and call
his mother's name, helplessly, whispering it as if he were worried
someone would hear him. How often she hoped he would make her
feel like a woman. "I wasn't just one woman," she said. "I was several
women all rolled into one. I was always starved for a big meal, and
all he gave me was crumbs."

Her feelings toward her husband must have been contagious, and they must have been transmitted to her daughter, who does not show her father the consideration he deserves as a father and who does not express toward her husband the affection he deserves as a husband.

I could not believe that my mother-in-law had not interfered in her daughter's pregnancy and that she was letting her do whatever she wanted, like going to the beach and risking her baby's safety. Was my wife taking the necessary precautions? Even I knew that a pregnant woman should be cautious at all times, and I did not even have any experience in this area. How could a woman who had given birth so many times not know that? Something was not right.

But, what was it?

Quite simply, my wife had had an abortion.

Oh, my God.

My aunt did not deny that she knew my wife had been pregnant. But she had remained silent when I asked her why she and my mother-in-law had acted as if they did not know every time I asked them about this issue. I had said things like: "How long can things stay in limbo?" "She's at the end of her second month of pregnancy, so how long is she planning to hide it?" "Is her belly round yet? Has she gained any weight?" "Have her friends told her that pregnancy suits her?"

Of course, none of these things happened because my wife had had an abortion—something that my aunt finally disclosed to me, after having kept it from me for an eternity of three long weeks. My wife had had the abortion, rested for a few days to regain her energy, and then left for the Gulf to visit her brothers there.

Oh, my God.

My aunt had not been overly concerned about the abortion. She had been more concerned with solving the problem between the seamstress's brother and me. Every time I called her she would ask me about whether or not I had resolved the issue. And, every time, I tried to reassure her that everything was fine—but she still was not reassured. She was so persistent that she was ready to pay for the settlement, no matter what the cost.

Lightning Source UK Ltd.
Milton Keynes UK
UKOW02f1808090615

253199UK00001B/42/P